The Banana Girls

The Banana Girls

Karim F Hirji

MKUKI NA NYOTA
DAR — ES — SALAAM

PUBLISHED BY
Mkuki na Nyota Publishers Ltd
P. O. Box 4246
Dar es Salaam, Tanzania
www.mkukinanyota.com

© Karim F Hirji, 2017

ISBN 978-9987-08-320-6

Visit www.mkukinanyota.com for information about and purchase of Mkuki na Nyota books.
Sign up for our e-news letter for updates on new releases and other announcements.

International Distributor:
African Books Collective
www.africanbookscollective.com

CONTENTS

To

The Fruit, Vegetable and Food Vendors of Dar es Salaam

Nourishing Millions with Delights

PREFACE

The stars of this book are two banana-addicted young girls driven by the spirit of inquiry, respect for the truth and humanistic idealism. As they navigate their eventful lives, an enticing tale of contrasts emerges: love and callousness, justice and injustice, scientific integrity and scholarly misconduct, the rich and the poor, national and international politics, and more. The emergent contradictions propel them far in the lands of ideas and action, to places none had ever dreamed about.

It is a work of fiction. Apart from a few prominent persons, its characters derive from my imagination. Any other resemblance to persons, alive or not, is coincidental. The tale also features three entities from the plant kingdom: bananas, groundnuts and the flamboyant tree. Songs and mathematical problems relating to bananas and related items are found here and there. In sum, it is a varied tapestry woven to entertain and inform.

The setting, though, reflects the current and historical reality in Africa and elsewhere, with the question of fair trade for the poor nations being a pressing one. The plight of the street sellers in African cities is a mammoth issue for which the investor oriented neo-liberal regimes have no solution but to vacillate between uneasy tolerance and merciless repression. These pages will hopefully illuminate such matters, and spark the desire to know more. The Supplementary Material is a guide in that direction.

With those words, I leave you to explore the multifaceted lives and adventures of the Banana Girls.

Karim F Hirji
June 2017

GLOSSARY

ahsante = thank you

andazi = fried sweet bun (plural mandazi)

askari = policeman, soldier or militia person

baba = father

bao = traditional board game

bibi = grandmother or elderly woman

chai = tea

dada = sister

daladala = city bus

kahawa = coffee

kaka = elder brother

karanga = groundnuts

kismavu ya nazi = cassava leaves in coconut sauce

kuku pilau = spiced rice with chicken

mama = mother

mama lishe = lady food vendor

matoke = plantain cooked with meat or beans

mkakaya = flamboyant tree, flame tree

mikokoteni = locally made large push cart

mtoto = child or baby

Mungu Wangu = God or Allah

mwalimu = teacher

mzee = elderly man

mzee nidizi tamu = sweet banana man (elder)

ndizi = banana or bananas

njugu = groundnuts

njugumawe = bambara nuts

nyama = meat

nyani = monkey

shairi = traditional Swahili poetry

shamba = farm

shikamo = greeting of respect

taarab = song and music from the East African coast

ugali = maize meal

uji = maize or grain porridge

ADDICTION

When and where does this story begin? It depends on your point of view.

Day -3230117: If you are in a historic frame of mind, you will trace it eight to ten thousand years ago to some islands off the coast of Asia. A roving band of humans for the first time found out that the fruit of an unusual plant they often encountered was edible. By what means remains a mystery; perhaps they were very hungry and just tried it out; perhaps they saw a monkey eating it.

The plant, about two times their height, had a soft stem that sprouted long, wide, singly-constituted green leaves. As it was, they had been putting two or three leaves side by side on level ground to make a sitting or sleeping mat. The cylindrically curved yellow-green fruit hung low in a bunch. Soft, sweet and filling, it boosted their energy. Soon it caught on.

Day -53117: If your outlook is narrower, you may start in the era when it began to feature in international trade and spread worldwide. You will come to observe that today there is no nation where it is not consumed. Rich in minerals and vitamins, a good source of dietary fiber, it comes in many varieties. Some are eaten as they ripen. Others are cooked in a diversity of cultural styles. Its history, production and sale signify global and local politics and history. In ways good and bad, some not that apparent, you will surmise that it embodies modern society.

Day 0000: The students and teachers at Batamaza Secondary School, however, are not in a reflective mood. With their focus on here and now, for them, the tale begins early today. Their school was built in the colonial era, seventy years ago. The walls obviously require a fresh coat of paint. Windows and blackboards need repair. But otherwise, it is well maintained. It has about six hundred students in Form I to Form VI.

The day has dawned with a light drizzle. Fatuma enters by the main gate. Her umbrella has signs of wear and tear. Rehema is waiting for her.

"You are wet, Fatuma."

"It is not much," she says with a smile.

Rehema hands her a handkerchief to dry her forehead, and the duo hurry towards the morning assembly area. The dark clouds are dispersing. The Emperor of the Heavens is asserting himself, projecting his life-giving rays on the greenery below. Students stand in rows, with Form I on the left and Form VI on the right. The two girls take their usual place, the front of the Form V line, next to each other.

Mr. Marufu, the headmaster, climbs onto the small wooden podium, beaming his stern gaze onto his wards. At his side there is a tall woman with spectacles and a white coat, like that you see in a hospital. She is new to the place. He raises his cane. A hushed silence prevails. He looks from left to right. Something catches his eye. Pointing his cane toward the back of the Form III row, he barks:

"You there, stop whispering among yourselves. Stand upright."

Now there is pin drop silence. Everyone stands erect.

"Good morning, girls and boys."

"*Shikamo, mwalimu.*" A loud response ensues.

After two routine announcements, he turns to the business of the day.

> "We are privileged today to have Dr. Sabria with us. She is our District Health Officer. She has important things to tell us. Listen carefully, all of you."

It was thirty-five years ago that he joined this place, as a biology and health studies teacher. A decade on, he was the headmaster. A short, stocky man, he walks upright, and at a brisk pace, casting a perceptive gaze at all the goings-on. Nothing escapes his attention. His demeanor reflects his personality, strict and demanding. In his hand, he sports a cane that he habitually waves about towards errant students. Yet he never administers corporal punishment, and forbids his staff to do it, too. A fair and considerate head, he just requires that each person do what he or she is supposed to do, and do it well. Despite his strictness, he is well liked.

Dr. Sabria has a gentle, friendly voice. Mr. Marufu hands her a megaphone. Her topic is making healthy food choices. She begins by posing questions:

> "How many of you drank bottled soda or juice yesterday? Raise your hand."

More than half the hands go up.

> "How many of you drank coconut water yesterday?"

Very few hands are up now.

> "How many of you had a sweet cake, biscuit or *andazi* yesterday?"

More than two-thirds of the students did.

> "How many of you had roasted corn or cassava?"

Only about a fifth did.

> The doctor surmises:

> "We have come to prefer factory made foods that are very sweet or salty, or fried foods. They are tasty but if you have them all the time, they can cause serious diseases. And we tend to avoid natural, wholesome foods that protect our health."

The students seem to be paying attention. But her instinct tells her that the majority are starting to tune out. So she describes a series of graphic cases of what happens to people who develop obesity, high blood pressure, diabetes and heart disease. The students are informed that these ailments are on the rise, even among young people.

"You can get addicted to junk food," she concludes. "Like cigarettes, it shortens a person's life."

Mr. Marufu has worried about these issues for a while. His students, though, mostly want to yawn. At the end of the short talk, only Rehema has a question for the doctor:

"When we go to the shops, we only find cakes, buns, soda, sweet juice, candies, potato chips and cookies. They are cheap and we like them. If they are not good for us, why is there nothing else? Why does the government allow the sale of this dangerous stuff to children? Why are there frequent announcements on the radio promoting these items?"

Dr. Sabria looks a bit taken back. After a short pause, she says:

"To tell you the truth, I have the same questions. I do not know the answer. As a doctor, it is my duty to warn you about the health dangers you face. I hope you will use this knowledge to make healthy choices in your lives."

Day 0001: Rehema and Fatuma are the best of buddies. Every day at break time, they sit under the expansive flamboyant tree in the yard.

"We need to make good choices," says Rehema.

Fatuma responds:

"But I can only bring bananas."

"The banana is a heathy fruit. I like it too. I think Dr. Sabria would approve. Still, we must investigate."

Day 0002: Having a scientific turn of mind, they shun idle speculation or superficial ideas. They seek facts and logic. The next day, they pore over books on nutrition in the school library. The librarian provides them relevant articles from the Internet.

They learn that bananas are a good source of vitamins B6 and C, and essential minerals like manganese, potassium and copper. They contain dietary fiber, which has multiple health benefits. Depending on the size, a ripe banana yields between 80 to 120 calories of energy. Even though they are sweet, bananas do not raise blood glucose level as much or as rapidly as sugary drinks. That is, they have a low glycemic index. Bananas promote the growth of healthy bacteria in the gut. It is a fruit, they discover, recommended by nutritionists. Some of what they read is not clear to them. They ask Mrs. Kamala, the biology teacher:

"*Mwalimu*, what is the glycemic index?"

"Our body breaks down the carbohydrates in our diet into glucose, which is our main source of energy. The glycemic index of a food item is a measure of how rapidly it increases the level of glucose in the blood. Regular sugar is given the index value of 100, and everything is compared to it."

"How does that affect our health?"

"If you want to make a five mile run or chop a big pile of firewood then a sweet drink will give you the needed energy. But if you have such sugary stuff frequently, the persistently high levels of glucose in the blood damages the body's regulatory system and predisposes you to chronic diseases."

"What about bananas?"

"Bananas are sweet but they contain fiber which slows down digestion. It is better to eat a banana than to eat a cream cake."

Day 0003: Satisfied that bananas are a healthy choice, and, for them, the most practical one, they arrive at what eventually will turn out to be a momentous decision:

Bananas it shall be.

Day 0017: It has been going on for about two weeks. At first, no one takes notice. A week on, the word spreads: These girls eat only bananas. Bananas, bananas, bananas: are they nutty?

Day 0019: *Mzee* Simon, the cleaner, mentions it to Mr. Marufu. He was the first to note the pattern: two or more banana peels lie in the trashcan next to the flamboyant tree each and every school day. The headmaster decides to check it out for himself. On his break time schoolyard tour, he makes it a point to pass near that tree. Sure enough, the girls are there, engrossed in a world of their own. Each has a banana in hand.

"Well, well," he mutters to himself. "I have seen kids take to cigarettes and worse. But bananas, that is a first. Do I have a problem with an addiction to bananas? Not really."

He scratches his shaggy chin as he merrily walks away in wonder.

If he had heard their talk, he would have been more perplexed. Mr. Felix, the mathematics teacher, has told them that the integer 1, even though it is only divisible by itself, is not a prime number. Fatuma concurs but Rehema has her doubts, hence their intense, though hushed, exchange.

Day 0029: The girls are odd. The teacher poses an easy question. All except them raise their hands. They simply look at each other. He asks a hard question. Only they raise their hands. One laughs, the other follows suit. On top of that, the questions they ask sometimes pose quite a challenge for the teacher.

The biology session today deals with flowers and pollination. What the students like about Mrs. Kamala is that she takes them on field trips every month. As the school has no budget for the trips, she has procured funding from an environmental organization. That day, they also get a packed lunch. Being a practice-oriented teacher, she generally brings specimens for the topic of the day to class. Last week, she brought a huge watermelon, which was carefully sliced to demonstrate the structure and components of the fruit, and each student had a tasty snack at the end of the session. Today she has five different types of flowers, including roses and rosellas.

At question time, Rehema holds up a flower she has collected during the break and asks:

"*Mwalimu*, the inner side of one petal of this flamboyant tree flower is white with reddish spots while the other four petals are uniformly pinkish red. Why is that so? Are there other flowers like that?"

Mrs. Kamala smiles as if to say "Why do you always have a tricky question, girl?" and replies:

"The scientific name for the flamboyant tree is *Delonix regia*. It is also known as Royal Poinciana, or flame tree. I am sure all of you have seen it in our schoolyard and elsewhere. People say it is one of the most beautiful plants. You have to see it in full bloom to appreciate its beauty."

She has everyone in the class examine the flower Rehema has in her hand.

"To answer your question: first, it should be realized that every fixed feature of a living organism has evolved over millions of years in order to give it some survival benefit. I do not exactly know why the flamboyant flower is so distinctive but I suspect it gives the specie some advantage. Perhaps it favorably attracts pollinators like bees and wasps. I do not think this matter has been investigated. I have not seen other flowers of that kind. Has anyone seen else?"

None of the students has.

"Does anyone know the Swahili name for the flamboyant tree?"

No one does. Even the Banana Girls do not raise their hands.

"It is *Mkakaya*."

Then, fervent environmentalist that she is, she makes a general observation:

"When I was your age, most parts of our city were dotted with flamboyant trees. Now there are fewer and fewer. In some areas, not a single tree remains. We cut down valuable marvels of nature and replace them with artificial things. This is but one example of the narrowing biodiversity in the plant and animal kingdoms that is taking place on all the continents. It is not a replaceable loss. Your children and their children are will not be able to see, touch or smell these magnificent things. They will have to be content with photos. And who knows what medicinal and useful properties they possess. Is that right? Think about that."

Now there is work for the class.

"Rehema, thank you for the excellent question. The assignment for the week is to locate flamboyant trees in your neighborhood. Draw, using color pencils and on plain paper, one tree and label its parts. If you have a cell phone, take one or two photos. If there is no *Mkakaya* where you stay, use the one in the schoolyard."

In the staff room, Mrs. Kamala reports:

"I like these two girls. They drive me beyond my usual mental limits but do it so gently. With their unpredictable inputs, other students become more attentive. I am sure the question they raised today will make their classmates look more closely at the structure of flowers."

Day 0031: The Banana Girls are inseparable. In class, they sit close up. If one plays basketball in PE, the other joins in. At break time, they huddle under the expansive flamboyant tree, whispering who knows what.

They do well in school work, but only in unison. Their favorite subjects are mathematics and physics. The physics lab session today is on magnetic fields. In the first experiment, they work separately. Both do a poor job. In the second one, they are paired. They outdo everyone else. During the free period, they tackle homework exercises jointly. But if anyone asks their help in these subjects, they are happy to oblige.

Day 0041: Look at them. Would you expect it? Rehema, short and chubby, has shiny black shoes; her uniform is spotlessly clean. Fatuma is tall and slim. Her once white blouse is a shade of grey. Her small left toe itches to push through the worn fabric of her shoe. When Fatuma finds something funny, her laughter emerges in loud ripples. Her handshake is vigorous and firm. Her friend displays a broad grin, and takes your hand in a nimble, lady like manner. Rehema comes to school by the *daladala*. For Fatuma, it is a long walk. Yet, they are never late.

Day 0043: To them, none of it matters. What others mutter behind their backs does not bother them. What matters is their companionship and what they have at break time. Each day, as it has been for about a while now, it must be bananas. Today, Fatuma has brought a succulent, green banana. It is a big one. Rehema has with her two small yellow bananas.

Yesterday, while helping her mother in the kitchen, Fatuma had asked:

"*Mama*, can't we eat banana skins?"

At first, her mother had ignored her. But when the question was repeated, *Mama* began to laugh. But then she responded, in an apologetic tone:

"I am sorry, my dear, I did not mean to make fun of you. But your questions are so strange! Even monkeys do not eat them. Your *Baba* tells me not to throw them away. He feeds the skins to the goats and chicken in the neighbor's yard or buries them in his *shamba*. They fertilize the soil."

"But I read in a book that you can eat banana skins."

"That is the problem, my dear. You are always reading books. You cannot believe everything you read. You also have to learn from your elders. Listen more carefully to your *Baba* and your uncles. They know many useful things."

And that was the end of that. Of late, both the girls had been getting similar responses from their parents. They would pose a query they considered reasonable, yet in the eyes of their parents, it was not. They usually got admonishing looks and dismissive replies.

Day 0053: Once each week Fatuma brings a freshly roasted plantain. Today Rehema has a reddish brown banana. While Fatuma's menu is more fixed, she sports a varied fare. One day this, the next day that. At times, it is a green one, and then, a day-old fried plantain.

Day 0059: Whatever it is, they share it equally. If there is an extra one, they give it to another student. Today, they give a nice yellow one to Jonathan, who is sitting nearby.

Later, they are in the school library, looking for university-level mathematics textbooks. Finding two copies of one such book on the shelf, each checks one out. The librarian knows them as her top borrowers. Atypically preferring books over cell phones, they seem like holdovers from an ancient era.

Day 0071: By now, they are called the Banana Girls, even by Mr. Marufu. He is proud of them. They are his model students. In the morning assembly, he lauds their good conduct, diligence, punctuality and exemplary performance.

Yet they do not arouse envy. Their humility and simplicity puts them in the good books of all. It is as if their presence generates a psychological force field that orients other students onto a studious pathway. The teachers love them as well.

However, some students at times make them the butt of crude jokes.

"Why do lions not eat bananas?"

"Because, they would rather eat a banana girl."

Or:

"What happened to the monkey who ate a whole bunch of bananas?"

"It went bananas."

Today, a creative fellow draws, in good spirits, a picture on the chalkboard just before the first period, which is Mr. Felix's mathematics period.

$$\beta(\alpha n)^2\alpha = $$

Like everyone else, the Banana Girls are amused by the artful drawing. Yet, they also see a major flaw. When Mr. Felix comes in, he too has the same reaction.

"Can anyone point out an error with this equation?" He asks.

Only the Banana Girls raise their hands.

"Sir, suppose you write the left hand side this way:

$$\beta\alpha^3 n^2$$

then algebraically, it is unchanged. But it is not a banana anymore."

James protests:

"Sir, it is just a joke. Can we not leave algebra and logic out of it?"

Rehema retorts:

"Even jokes should have a logical basis."

Mr. Felix resolves the dispute:

"Both of you have a point. Now let us turn to the lesson of the day."

Day 0073: When the students enter the classroom, they find the following problem on the blackboard. Mr. Felix guesses who has put it there.

Banana Problem 1

Fatima is walking home with a lion, a monkey and a bunch of bananas. Halfway there, she has to cross a river. The small boat can take only one of the three. The monkey cannot be left with the bananas and the lion cannot be left with the monkey. How can she make the crossing?

The Banana Girls had stayed on after class time the previous day to put it there. Only a few students work out the solution (see the Banana Mathematics section). With a smirk on their faces, Fatuma and Rehema explain it. The next morning, the blackboard reads:

If you do not eat bananas,
you will go bananas.

The Banana Girls have the last laugh. In any case, they do not feel isolated or offended if people make fun of them. They have gathered from their readings that you get bananas, be it from a farm, vendor, shop or market, in almost all parts of the world, and they are the most consumed of all the fruits. Can you feel alone or downcast when you are a conscious, active member of a family numbering in the billions?

Day 0079: The rainy season is in full swing. Fatuma, with her rickety umbrella, always manages to arrive at school in time. But not today: she is fifteen minutes late. The teacher at the gate takes her to Mr. Marufu's office.

Usually the head would loudly admonish a late arrival, but he knows that this girl must have a good reason. He asks gently:

"Did you have a problem at home?"

"Yes, I had to help *Baba*. Our roof was leaking."

"I see. You can go now."

It is the first time a Banana Girl has been late. Her classmates treat her with sympathy. Mr. Felix places a gentle hand on her shoulder. The class proceeds as if nothing is amiss.

Yet it is a distinctively strange day in another way too. The girls talk to each other in a loud voice at break time. Each has a stick she uses to draw lines on the ground. They point fingers at one another. The majestic flame tree feels ill at ease. Later, they are withdrawn, pensive. What were they arguing about? A sense of mystery pervades the school.

Day 0083: Mr. Felix explains the incident to Mr. Marufu.

> "They were discussing whether the cardinality of the set of even numbers is the same as the cardinality of the set of integers. It is a paradox of infinite sets. An actual part of the whole can nonetheless be equivalent to the whole."
>
> "Do not talk meaningless stuff to me. Are they doing fine?"
>
> "Oh yes, it is a vexing issue but finally they agreed that the cardinality of the two sets is identical. Now both are as cheerful as ever."
>
> "That is all I want to know."

Day 0239: Time has flown by. The girls are in Form VI, enjoying their final year in high school. Last month, *Baba* Fatuma was able to buy a new uniform for his daughter. And she walks in comfort since her uncle gave her a good pair of shoes.

Oral presentations are an annual tradition in Mr. Felix's senior class. In the middle of the school year, students in groups of two or three work on a project and make their presentations to the class. There are two requirements. The project should have a numerical aspect and demonstrate a creative angle.

James and Julia have just concluded their presentation, which was entitled:

*A mathematical formula for the leaf of
the Flamboyant tree flower.*

They employed two-dimensional polar coordinates to model the outer boundary of such a leaf. To gauge the accuracy of their model, they superimposed ten leaves onto the theoretical outline, and showed the resulting photos. In seven instances, the fit was impressive.

Now it is Rehema and Fatuma's turn. Their project sounds weird:

How many groundnuts did Mzee Salum sell at our school?

Yet it instantly resonates with the whole class.

First they ask the class to make a reasonable guess. A few say it is not possible to answer the question. Another group has the number between 200,000 to 500,000 nuts; and another bolder group, between two billion to ten billion nuts. The girls then give their answer:

"From his first day to his last, it is reasonable to say that *Mzee* Salum sold 180,000,000 groundnuts at this school."

The class is astonished.

"How can you ever know?"

They explain the process through which they have obtained this number.

Until recently, every school day, students would rush during the break towards the main gate. Just outside, vendors sold roasted maize, sweet potato and cassava plus fruits (oranges, tangerines, bananas, pineapple slices) as well as roasted *karanga*, popcorn, *njugumawe* and sweets. *Mzee* Salum had sold roasted groundnuts here for forty years, from a time even before Mr. Marufu joined the school.

His freshly roasted nuts were a prized commodity, selling out in minutes. One packet was always reserved for Mr. Marufu; his secretary would come to collect it.

While the Banana Girls had their own daily snack, once a week Rehema bought a packet of nuts from him. One odd day, with their numerical turn of mind, they decided that the nuts should be divided absolutely equally between them. From then on, whenever they got a packet, they literally counted the nuts and split the lot equally. And they kept a record.

The lowest number of whole nut equivalents in the twelve packets they had counted was 235; the highest was 245. Each packet was worth 200 shillings. Rehema asked *Mzee* Salum about the value of the nuts he sold in a day. He said it varied from 14,000 to 15,000 shillings, implying that his daily sale was roughly 70 to 75 packets. In addition, they figured that he came to the school 250 to 270 days every year, and noted that he had done this for forty years.

Though the price per packet, like that of all else, had risen over the years, he informed them that two things did not: the quality of his nuts and the packet size. The number of packets he sold per day hardly varied either.

Using the lower and higher numbers separately, they calculated that per year, *Mzee* Salum had sold between 165 million and 200 million groundnuts at this school. 180 million, the center of this range was taken as a reasonable estimate for the grand total. They clarify that their numbers are rounded to the nearest five million.

The class listens attentively. Mr. Felix praises their creative, scientific approach. James has a question.

"How many nuts do you think he would have sold?"

Though his wording is vague, the class understands exactly what he has in mind.

"We had expected this question. Two months back, *Mzee* Salum told us that after five years, he was going to retire to his home village, 120 miles from here. If you extend the sale years from 40 to 45, and extrapolate our number, you get 200,000,000 nuts."

"So our school has been deprived of 20 million nuts."

"Yes, that is what we think: 20 million missing nuts."

After class, they tell Mr. Felix that they could have obtained better estimates using mean and standard deviation. But since their sample size was only twelve packets, and that it was not a random sample, there was no point in doing fancy calculations. These days many experts bandy about flawed figures obtained from poor research design which is masked by the use of complex formulas. Mr. Felix is struck by the scientific integrity and erudite take on statistics of these girls.

Day 0241: When the word of this juggling of numbers reaches Mr. Marufu, via Mr. Felix of course, his initial reaction is:

"Have the girls gone nuts?"

But then he ruefully reflects:

"Of those 20 million, what would have been my share?"

The reason the issue resonates widely is that the vendors are no more. It happened like a bolt out of the blue a couple of weeks ago. The new mayor has decreed a city-wide ban on hawkers and street vendors. He says they bring chaos and lawlessness to the city and damage its reputation as a clean and orderly place. It may drive tourists away. As a part of this campaign, vendors selling food items at the gate of Batamaza school were chased away by the city militia. Everyone recalls that for a few days after that day, the headmaster had been moody and abrupt, both with the staff and students. The smallest cause sufficed to make him snap at anyone nearby. It was uncanny. Only his secretary knew the reason: these were the withdrawal blues emanating from his addiction to *Mzee* Salum's delightful nuts. To the school's relief, he was his normal self within a week.

REVELATION

Day 0271: For the students at Batamaza school, it is an anxiety-laden day. The teachers hand out the results of the mid-term tests. Happy and sullen faces prevail. The Banana Girls are tied at the top of the Form VI class. Fatuma is the highest scorer in mathematics, followed closely by Rehema. In physics, it is the other way around. That is the usual story. Because the girls always sit next to each other, Mr. Marufu had initially suspected foul play. But the outcome does not change even if they do the examinations in separate rooms. Are they mutually telepathic?

The math test was for calculus, with the focus on integration by parts and optimization. To lighten the mood, Mr. Felix had set a banana problem as the first problem.

Banana Problem 2

The hungry *Baba Nyani* enters the kitchen at night and eats 1/6 of a banana bunch. At dawn, *Mama Nyani* feasts on 1/5 of what remains. *Kaka Nyani* gobbles up 1/4 of what he finds upon return from work, and *Dada Nyani* is satisfied with 1/3 of what is there. *Mtoto Nyani* is content with half of what is left for him. After he has had his share, 7 bananas remain. How many bananas were there at the outset?

It is a primary school problem, but it reduces tension. Rehema and Fatuma issue a low chuckle. Surprisingly, that boastful guy who makes fun of the girls gets it wrong (The answer is 42; see the Banana Mathematics section.)

For the two, today is a special day, but for another reason. At break time, they make a solemn pact and promise each other that they will remain friends for life, even after they get married and have children. And they will help each other secure the highest possible level of education.

Later, they are in a pretty jolly mood. Others wonder: is it that scoring high in the exams has finally made them big headed? They could not be more mistaken.

Day 0311: It is the early hours of a cloudy, windy day. Fatuma has had her bowl of maize *uji*. She wants to rush off to school. Yet, she is upset.

"*Mama*, there is no banana here. Have you roasted a plantain?"

"I am sorry, my baby. *Baba* did not harvest anything this morning."

"Why? Is he still in the *shamba*?"

"No my dear, he is asleep. He is unwell. He was injured at work. He came home so late."

"*Baba* is injured!" Fatuma screams.

She and seven year old Ali sleep in the front room of their two-room dwelling, a mud-walled tin-roofed shack. The cooking area is outdoors. Behind it is their acre-and-a-half banana farm. Most trees yield the plump, sweet green variety; the others, longish plantains. There are a few papaya and lime trees together with corn stalks interspersed throughout the *shamba*.

Baba cuts off a bunch of bananas each morning. Leaving a good one on the mat for Fatuma, he carries the rest in a basket for sale at the city center. On days of no harvest, he buys a bunch from an adjacent farm and sells it. But the profit margin in that case is low.

His bananas are highly valued in the neighborhoods he frequents. It is only on a rare day that he does not return with an empty basket. Though he is barely forty, they call him *Mzee Ndizi Tamu* (Sweet Banana Old Man).

At times, he gets a special order on his barely functional cell phone for a large bunch of plantains for a wedding or a special event. He then hires a *mikokoteni* to make the delivery.

Rain or shine, he has never failed to keep aside a banana for the jewel of his eyes.

Fatuma trudges to school in a sour mood. Those dark bruises on *Baba*'s face and arms – what happened? Feeling the void in her bag, she sneaks into the classroom quietly, with barely a nod to her best friend. Though she is a minute late, the teacher does not say anything.

At break time, Rehema wonders:

"What is wrong? I have never seen you like this, Fatuma."

"My *Baba* is sick, and I have no banana for you."

"I am so sorry to hear about your *Baba*. The doctor's medicine will soon make him well."

"We have no money for a doctor. *Mama* gave him a Panadol. He was in so much pain."

"Oh. But don't worry about bananas. I have three today, and they are just like the ones you bring."

For Rehema, the day had started with the usual argument with her *Mama*.

"Wake up, Rehema. Today you can take two apples to school, one for you and one for your friend. Or you can take two *mandazi*."

"No. I want bananas, only bananas."

"You stubborn girl. Well, you are in luck today. Yesterday evening, your *baba* brought home a big bunch. They are so delicious."

As Rehema recounts her verbal tussle with her *Mama*, Fatuma is surprised.

"I thought you had a big *shamba*. Why does your *Baba* have to buy bananas?"

"You silly goose, whoever gave you the idea. My *Baba* is a sergeant in the city militia. He catches the bad guys, those who break the law. When he returns from work, he buys bananas for me. He knows I love them. I love my *Baba*."

Fatuma is quiet.

"I am not sure, though."

"Why?"

"Once I heard him tell *Mama* that he gets fruits and vegetables when he chases the bad guys. Often they panic and leave their stuff behind. I think that is how he got the big bunch yesterday."

For a week, the girls are worried and withdrawn. Fatuma and her *Mama* pick the bananas from the *shamba*. Mama keeps the lot in the front porch for sale to passersby. Usually, a half or more remains unsold. For a few days, the family mostly has banana-based meals. The day her *Baba* is out of bed, Fatuma's spirits rise. And that uplifts Rehema's spirits as well.

Day 0337: *Baba* has resumed his banana sales. But he has to do it surreptitiously to evade the militia patrols. He has located several places along his route where he can hide his stuff in case they come around.

The girls resume their routine, and are seen as their happy selves once again. A collective sigh of relief spreads across the school. The innocence, charm, diligence and creativity of the Banana Girls have come, as much as the steadfast leadership of Mr. Marufu, to symbolize the spirit of the Batamaza school.

Day 0373: Mr. Marufu has a major problem in mind. He worries about the rising level of indiscipline among the students. Today, he issues a warning during morning assembly, replaying a part of the President's recent speech on the loudspeakers.

Too many of our youth have become lazy. They play pool, drink, do drugs or break the law. We cannot tolerate this anymore. If they do not change their habits, they will be sent to the rural areas to work on farms. No loafers shall loiter in our streets anymore.

Rehema is pleased to hear this. She thinks to herself:

"My *Baba* is implementing the President's policy by catching the bad guys. He is a good man. But I hope he will drink less beer. He is not kind to *Mama* sometimes."

Fatuma is lost in her own thoughts:

> "My *Baba* works so hard, from morning to evening. People love his bananas. He is not a loafer. I hope nothing will happen to my *Baba*. During vacation time, I will help him clear weeds from the farm."

The Mayor of the city has given his own interpretation of those words. According to him, the hawkers and vendors who sell their wares where they please, operate without a license, do not pay taxes and clog up the streets are also to be dispatched to the rural areas.

Tussles between the city authorities and street sellers have gone on for as long as people can remember. And it always is a cyclical affair. One day, the city officials institute a crackdown; the streets are cleared; three to four months later, the sellers are back. It is back to business as usual.

This time around, there is a difference. The new President wants all policies to be implemented in a thorough manner. So the crackdown is far-reaching. It matters not if you spread your wares on the pavement of a busy street or if you go door to door with your fruits, you are a target of the vast dragnet. In the past, vendors selling food items near schools had been spared. This time, no exceptions are made. One fine morning, a militia van zoomed up to the gate of Batamaza school just as the sellers had taken their positions. Some were caught. The fate of *Mzee* Salum is not known. The area outside the school gate has remained barren since then.

No student or teacher comments on the speech. They return to class to do what they always do. But everyone's mind is on the same thing:

> "Were the vendors the loafers the President was talking about? Have they all been dispatched to rural villages? Where is *Mzee* Salum? Those 20 million nuts: will we ever get to enjoy them?"

These were the common, but unspoken thoughts in the school that day.

Day 0383: The flamboyant tree is in full bloom, a serenade of pink and red on its royal canopy. *Mzee* Simon has kept a fresh bunch of flowers for the girls near the trunk. Strangely, they take little notice. They have a fundamental issue to resolve. It generates another loud discussion. But now no one is worried. Mr. Felix explains it to Mr. Marufu.

"They were talking about the infinitude of paired primes."

"Is that something immoral? You know what these kids get from the Internet these days."

"Oh no, sir. It is a famous unresolved mathematical problem."

"Not again. But I hope one day they become famous scientists. It will make our school famous too."

Day 0419: The final Form VI examination is around the corner. A good result is necessary for admission to university. The girls begin preparing in earnest. As he well knows their need to work together, Mr. Marufu allows them to stay on for an hour after class. Their parents have consented provided they come home immediately afterwards. Fatuma's *Mama* does not like it, but as her *Baba* has no objection, her opinion does not count.

Day 0421: Today, in a meeting with the headmasters of area schools, a proposal to set up small shops within the schoolyard is brought up. The shops will sell soda, packet juice, cookies, cakes and chips to the students. The district education office is negotiating with a businessman who will get the contract to run all the shops in a standard manner. While others are inclined to accept this offer, he has his doubts. If he consents, will not his students and staff deem him a hypocrite? Can he turn into a purveyor of harmful junk food?

After the meeting, a colleague tells him that the businessman in question is the brother-in-law of the city Mayor. He returns to his school in a sour mood, daydreaming about the sumptuous, missing 20 million groundnuts.

Day 0439: Done with their work, Fatuma walks her friend to the bus stop. They discuss a tricky point regarding integration by parts.

As they wait to cross the road, a city jeep passes by. Four hefty militia fellows in green uniform are standing at the back. Rehema is excited. Pointing to the man with two stripes on his upper right arm, she exclaims,

"Look, look, that is **my** *Baba*."

But Fatuma's gaze is directed at the man squatting at their feet; bloodied, with one eye closed. His clothes are torn.

"That is **my** poor *Baba*."

Day 0440: Amidst the cloudy gloom, the sun struggles to come up. Atypically, the red headed rooster sounds subdued as well.

"Rehema, you are late, wake up."

"I have fever. I am not going to school."

Mama touches her forehead.

"You are just fine. Have your tea, bread, jam and egg, and you will feel good."

"No, my legs hurt. I have a headache. I am not going to school."

The girl refuses to budge from her bed. To entice her stubborn child, *Mama* says,

"*Baba* has brought so many nice bananas for you. You can take four to school today."

"No, no, no. I hate bananas."

Her *Mama* cannot believe what she hears.

At her friend's place, another scene unfolds.

"Fatuma, your uncle is here. He says *Baba* is in police custody. We need fifty thousand shillings to have him released."

"So much money! Do you have it?"

"He will give us thirty thousand. I will get ten thousand shillings on loan from *Mzee* Saidi. We cannot access the money on *Baba's* cell phone account. So we have to raise the rest."

"How?"

"We will go to town to sell bananas. I know where your *Baba* goes. You will come with me."

"It is so dangerous, *Mama*."

"We will hide some in your school bag. And I will carry some in my cloths bag. No one will know."

At school all are perplexed. The flamboyant tree has been shedding its colorful bounty. But there is no one to appreciate it. When the report reaches Mr. Marufu, he knits his eyebrows, and is silent for a minute.

"That is very strange."

"Yes, so strange."

Then he has an insight.

"But it makes sense. They do everything together. So if one is absent, the other will be absent too. It makes sense."

Everyone concurs.

"Yes, it makes sense."

Day 0443: A most unusual day. Only Rehema is at school. She does not talk to anyone, and does not raise her hand as she usually did before. At break time, she remains in class, staring out of the window. She chews an *andazi* but does not touch the packet of honey-glazed nuts her *Mama* has put in her bag. Out there, the flamboyant tree shivers with loneliness. Its flower petals fall slowly, as if reluctantly, to the ground.

This time, the school does not need to wait for Mr. Marufu's verdict.

Everyone knows.

"It does not make any sense."

Mr. Felix expresses it in his own way to his class.

"Can you unpair a prime pair? Will the components still be prime?"

The physics teacher muses aimlessly.

"Can you magnetize a banana? Will it still be a banana?"

It sounds gibberish to the students. Yes it is, pure melancholic gibberish. Have the teachers gone bananas?

Mr. Marufu is in a state of shock. He makes a fateful decision.

"I have been at this place for thirty-five years. I am getting old, too old. Life is changing so fast. The computers, cell phones and new stuff, they are beyond me. As soon as the exams are over, I will file my application for retirement. I need to spend more time with my grandchildren."

Nonetheless, he is apprehensive. The Mayor has announced that city officials will conduct a house-to-house search to catch those who are not doing gainful, legal work.

"Will they brand me a loafer? Maybe I should wait for a while. You never know, I may be sent to a distant rural village."

At the moment, he has an immediate priority. He must find out what is happening to his star student. Rehema has not said anything and *Baba* Fatuma's cell phone does not connect anymore.

"I will pass by her house after school and find out."

Is the number of atoms in a banana greater than the number of stars in the universe? Is it greater than 20 trillion? Let the Banana Girls figure that out.

Mr. Marufu, for his part, is dead certain about one thing.

The smiles of the Banana Girls are sweeter than the sweetest banana in the universe.

Day 0449: With Mr. Marufu's financial assistance, *Baba* Fatuma was released from police custody yesterday. He was haggard and emaciated, barely able to stand or talk. *Mama* washed his hands and face with warm water, placed him on his chair and fed him hot *uji*. Without uttering a word, he then lay down on the mat, and slept like a log for six hours.

At dinner time, he touched the faces of his children, asking them how they were doing at school. *Mama* had prepared a big meal of rice and curry with the half a kilo of meat and a kilo of rice the neighbor had sent them.

Ali's first words were:

"*Baba*, they send thieves and crooks to jail. But you have done nothing bad. Why did they lock you up?"

"My son, it is because of politics. Our leaders do not like small traders like me. They are allied with big business. They just want to make life difficult for us."

"What did you do in jail, *Baba*?"

"Nothing, just nothing. Life was bad. The food was either hard like a stone or just watery. I had a stomachache throughout the day. I couldn't sleep. The floor was cold. Big cockroaches crawled everywhere. We were twenty five persons crowded in one room. Some were rough fellows. They cursed and fought with others. The police guards didn't do anything to stop the fights. They only laughed and walked away."

When Fatuma told him that she and Ali had weeded the *shamba* last weekend, his face lit up. Other than naming those who had assisted the family, *Mama* remained quiet but made sure everyone ate well. This morning, *Baba* looked much better. The first thing he did was to get two large bananas from the *shamba* for his daughter.

Fatuma enters the schoolyard with noticeably bright spirits. Hugging her best friend, she proclaims:

"*Baba* is home, Rehema, my *Baba* is home."

The day witnesses a sea change in the demeanor of the Banana Girls. Their talkative selves once again, they laugh aloud at the smallest cause. Noticed by students and teachers, the word spreads. Soon everyone is smiling and joking. The usually somber Mr. Marufu cannot help in breaking out in guffaw now and then.

The girls resume their exam preparation. They have lost much time and need to work harder.

Day 0503: It is the day for the release of the exam results. An anxious bunch of former Form VI students has returned to the school to know their fate. After pinning the results on the notice board, the headmaster calls a noontime assembly, something he rarely does.

"This is a very special day for our school. Fatuma has attained the highest rank in the National Form VI examination, and Rehema is the second highest person."

Loud cheers and claps break out. The girls hug each other. Mr. Marufu calls them to the podium and shakes their hands. Later the Banana Girls venture into the yard to say goodbye to *Mzee* Simon and their favorite tree. They also renew their compact.

"We will not allow anything to come between us, no matter what it is. We will remain the best friends for life."

The leaves and branches of the *mkakaya* flutter in the slow wind. Sad and forlorn though it is, it is nodding in approval.

Day 0521: The girls have been summoned to the Ministry of Education. Because of their outstanding performance, they have been awarded full scholarships to study at prominent universities abroad. When they get the application forms, they see that one of them will go to a British university and the other, to an American university.

They are taken aback. Do they want to be apart for the next three to four years? No, certainly not. They tell the Ministry official that they need to consult their parents, which of course is not the actual reason. He is shocked. Anyone else would have jumped at the golden opportunity. They are told that the forms need to be filled in by the next day.

When they return the following morning, they hand back the blank forms to the official and inform him that both of them would like to study at the National University. He is too confounded to ask why and just wishes them well.

Mr. Marufu and Mr. Felix too are flabbergasted when they come to know their decision. Yet they know that wherever the girls pursue their higher education, both will attain the pinnacle of excellence in their fields.

ILLUMINATION

Day 0641: Rehema and Fatuma are in their first year of studies at the National University. The former is training to be a physics teacher; the latter, a mathematics teacher. The vast campus, lush with greenery and open spaces, lies seven kilometers from the city center atop a gently sloped hill.

Each has a full scholarship that covers tuition and other costs. Unlike most students, they do not need a study loan. Rehema stays in a student dorm, but Fatuma resides at home to take care of Ali. Her *Mama*, who now is a domestic servant in the city center, leaves early for work every day except Sunday. Fatuma gives her brother breakfast and gets him ready for school. Then she walks a mile and a half to the university. On return, she boards a jam-packed *daladala*.

As close to each other as ever, the girls retain their taste for bananas, which Fatuma brings from her *shamba*. After lunch, they usually sit underneath the mid-sized *mkakaya* behind the cafeteria and savor their favorite fruit.

Day 0643: Fatuma's *Baba* has lost much of his vision in one eye. He does not go out to sell bananas anymore. Instead, a fruit marketing company sends a truck to his *shamba* once a week to purchase his harvest. The quality fruit is sold to tourist hotels for a hefty price but his income is lower than what it was in the earlier times. The buyer sets the price with no room for negotiation. Once a month or so, *Mama* takes a small bunch for her boss. Luckily, she gets a good price. The family struggles to make ends meet. *Baba*, who often has nothing to do these days, despairs at being turned into a loafer.

Ten years back, with the help of *Mama* Fatuma, he used to brew banana beer for sale. It was a popular product as attested to by the long line of eager customers that formed in the backyard each evening. And it was a steady source of good income. But he had to cease after the sale of any form of local brew was forbidden by the city health officer. He is thinking about resuming that business but *Mama* Fatuma is set against it. The risk is too great, she says. The entire family may suffer the consequences if he is caught.

Rehema's *Baba* has earned a promotion from his steadfast diligence clearing the city streets. Now a captain in the militia, three months ago, he returned from a four-week training at a police college in Texas, USA. He learned modern tactics of crowd control and the use of effective gear for the purpose. A batch of that gear was subsequently purchased by the city council from a US company. *Baba* had brought an elegant, expensive dress from Texas for his daughter. But she does not wear it.

Day 0659: Fatuma's subject combination is Pure Mathematics, Applied Mathematics and Education while Rehema studies Physics, Mathematics and Education. They attend the same lectures in Education and a few common mathematics courses. In addition, they attend the course that is required for all first year undergraduates, Development Studies.

Initially, they did not keenly follow the topics in this course. The presentations were rigid and dry. The lectures by Professor S Chachage of the Sociology Department, however, arouse their interest. His engaging oratory and material opens their eyes to the history and current realities of Africa and the World.

Day 0661: Astonishingly for the class, and particularly for the Banana Girls, his topic today is *The Global Political Economy of the Banana*. He begins by noting that while bananas currently grow in many parts of the world, it has not always been so. Originating in Asia, they landed in Africa some two thousand years ago and spread throughout the continent with the spread of Islamic culture. The Portuguese encountered them in the course of their African travels five centuries back, and took them to the Americas.

The bulk of the bananas, as in Africa, India and the Philippines, are eaten locally. But a good portion from some areas is for export, mainly to Europe, the US and Canada. And there lay a hidden aspect of the story. Professor Chachage informs them that the history of the banana trade over the past century is intimately connected to the present day inequality between the rich and poor nations. He demonstrates this by going over how large-scale banana cultivation began 150 years ago in Central and South America. American conglomerates like United Fruit seized vast tracts of land to set up huge banana plantations in places like Honduras and Guatemala. With the assistance of the US military, deceit and violence, they became the effective economic overlords of those lands. The firms involved in the growing, packaging, transport, and marketing reaped millions but paid little tax. Their *modus operandi* was to back dictatorial regimes that employed death squads and goons to maintain tight control over the super-exploited work force and silence oppositional voices. The workers toiled for long hours under hazardous, pesticide-laden conditions in return for low wages and no benefits. Thousands of activist workers, union leaders, journalists, intellectuals, students and even priests who stood up against corporate and state abuse were tortured, jailed or disappeared.

The historical examples given by Prof. Chachage are shocking. In Guatemala, an elected government was overthrown by the American CIA when it challenged the monopoly of American companies in a minor way. The dictatorship that took its place instituted a forty-year reign of terror that included genocidal pogroms against the indigenous population. That is the origin of the term "Banana Republic".

The legacy of that era persists. To this day, nearly four-fifths of the bananas grown in those nations are exported to provide cheap nourishment for the North American consumers. The same companies, under changed names, dominate the entire process. Yet, in the producer nations, you witness wide levels of social and state violence, gross economic inequality, mass unemployment, enduring poverty, child malnutrition, and widespread environmental degradation. Veritably, the tale of the American banana trade is a tale of toil, tears and terror.

The eyes of Fatuma and Rehema are watery as the professor ends this part of his lecture by screening a few photos of life in those nations.

In the second hour, he tells the class that in addition to the Banana Republics, bananas are also exported from the nations of the Caribbean, Pacific and Africa. These former colonies sell mainly to Britain and Europe. As with many commodities, the trade had begun during the harsh colonial days. But there was a difference. While the transport and marketing was dominated by external companies, banana cultivation was done on locally-owned small and medium-scale farms.

In the recent years, these nations had secured a better deal for their bananas as compared to the nations dominated by US companies. The basic conditions of inequality and dependency were, however, unchanged. The US government, moreover, contested this arrangement in the World Trade Organization. He notes that the important issue for Africa, in relation to bananas and other exports, is not free trade but fair trade.

Professor Chachage concludes by handing out excerpts of a few chapters from relevant books. These are required readings. Additionally, he says that two copies of *Bananas: How the United Fruit Company Shaped the World* by P Chapman and *Bitter Fruit: The Story of the American Coup in Guatemala* by S Schlesinger and S Kinzer are in the library reserve section. These are recommended but not required readings.

Once the class is over, the girls rush to the library. Each sits in a corner, a copy of one of the two books in hand. So engrossed are they for the next three hours that they miss a lecture on education and nearly miss their lunch. This scene is repeated for the next four days until each has read both the books.

Day 0673: The girls knock at the door of Professor Chachage's office and enter.

"Professor, we have a few questions."

"Sure."

Rehema begins:

"First, we want to say that we find your lectures very educative and fascinating. We think all students in Africa should learn that material."

"Thank you."

"We are wondering why you are the only lecturer who teaches this type of material?"

"Well, there are two others; one in the School of Law and one in History Department. But you are basically correct. Ninety-nine percent of the university instructors today avoid exploring such issues."

"Why?"

The girls are perplexed. He elaborates:

"Thirty years ago, the presentation of critical and analytic ideas was more common on this campus. But now the political climate has changed in a fundamental way. Now the intellectuals only praise the capitalist system and promote its values and ideas. They regard the Western nations as the saviors of Africa. The agencies from these nations provide them consultancy and project funds. So somehow they feel beholden to them."

"But that is not right!" The girls exclaim.

"A university education is not as objective as it is proclaimed to be. It is constrained by the dominant social system."

"Then what can we do?"

"In our days, we faced the same dilemma. Our answer was: educate yourself. At this age, you have attained a sufficient level of intellectual maturity to do likewise."

"Thank you, professor. We will follow your guidance."

"But feel free to come to me if you have questions. I suggest you begin your independent intellectual journey with Walter Rodney's *How Europe Underdeveloped Africa*. This is the most important book on African history written in the past hundred years and it was written right on this campus."

When she reaches home that evening, as is usually the case, Ali takes Fatuma's hand to take her into the backyard.

"*Dada, dada,* let us play."

Invariably, her response is:

"First, I have to arrange my things. Then I have to see if you have finished your homework."

Having done that, the play begins. Depending on Ali's mood, it is a game of catch with the almost worn out tennis ball *Baba* had got for him, drawing designs in the sand, shooting marbles, or just sitting and chatting. Often it is a mix. At times, Ali brings out the sturdy soccer ball Fatuma recently purchased for him from her lodging allowance money. Then they kick the ball to and fro. However, Ali prefers to reserve it for weekend football games with his friends in the neighborhood.

Day 0683: Today they are back in the professor's office. They seek clarification about the Banana War between the African, Caribbean and Pacific (ACP) nations, on the one hand, and the Latin American nations, on the other. At issue are the terms of trade for banana exportation.

The professor clarifies that though it appears to be a conflict between two groups of poor nations, it actually is a tug-of-war between Europe and the US to secure the best deal for their own companies and consumers. At the end of his long but illuminating explanation, Fatuma has a point:

"It sounds similar to what the big merchant is doing to my *Baba.* He buys our bananas at a low price and then sells them at a high price to the tourist hotels. *Baba* does all the hard work but the big man gets most of the profits. And *Baba* has no other choice; his avenue for getting a better deal has been blocked by the city council."

The professor concurs:

"You are so right. The workers and farmers of the poor nations are exploited, not just by international companies but also by the local capitalists and state authorities. That is how globalization, which is another name for the international capitalist system, works."

He has another point:

"The irony is that while Western nations have benefited a lot from our bananas, they have at the same time used this wonderful fruit to express racist sentiments towards Africans."

The girls wonder what he means.

"In the 1960s and 1970s, when European football clubs started to recruit talented players from Africa, it generated quite a bit of resentment, especially from the fans of the opposing teams. They called African players "monkeys", made monkey like noises, and threw bananas at them."

"Does that still happen?"

"Unfortunately, such ugly incidents continue to be reported from Western Europe and more so from Eastern Europe. At times, soccer officials are seen making racist comments. The rise of xenophobic, anti-immigrant tendencies in the West will magnify such behavior."

It was news to Fatuma and Rehema, who had thus far kept a distance from cultural and sports affairs and activities. And now the professor has a question for them:

"Have you heard of Harry Belafonte?"

"No, sir. Who is he?"

"Well, well. Now he is in his eighties, and is not so active. But in the 1960s and 1970s, he was one of the most popular singers in the world. Originally from Jamaica, he launched his musical career in the US. With an exquisite voice, his specialty was calypso songs."

"What are calypso songs?"

"That is not easy for me to explain. You have to listen to it to appreciate it. The reason why I mention him is that one of his most popular songs is the *Banana Boat Song*."

The girls' eyes widen.

"Is that so?"

"Yes, and it derives from the chants of banana workers. I have put three of his famous songs, the *Banana Boat Song, Island in the Sun* and *Jamaica Farewell*, in an audio format on this flash drive. You can copy them on your computer and listen to them."

"Thank you, thank you."

(The lyrics of the *Banana Boat Song*, also known as *Day-o*, appear in the Banana Culture section.)

They exit his office in an elated mood. Rehema has a laptop computer. Instead of heading to the library, they spend two hours in her dorm room, listening to the three songs, over and over.

After a while, they sing along, swinging their heads and bodies with the rhythm. If other students had seen them, they would have been astonished. Until now, these two girls had shown no interest in music, song or dance. They found the loud, fast paced and almost incoherent English and Swahili songs that were popular on the campus rather distasteful.

They liked the older *taarab* songs and *shairi* but these were rarely heard on any radio station nowadays. Fatuma had grown up with such music. When she was young, her father used to take her to the neighbor's place on weekends. He played *bao* and drank *kahawa* while she got tea and biscuits. An aging cassette player elicited soothing sounds of Islamic verse, *taarab* or *shairi*. *Baba* would recite these at home. Fatuma had introduced them to Rehema when they were at Batamaza school.

Once they came across two boys from their class engrossed in a fast paced song. The volume was high but the words were hard to make out. They inquired:

"What is this song?"

"It is African rap, baby."

"What does it say?"

"You are so dumb. Everyone knows *Ukombozi* (Liberation). It has been at the top of the charts for a month now."

"Liberation for whom?"

"For Africa, man!"

"And, liberation from what? What kind of charts are you talking about – pie-charts or graphs?"

"Man-o-man, so many silly questions. You are not in a science class. Be cool, babies. Listen to the rap, and enjoy the beat. It's kinda groovy."

Unable to make head or tail of what they were being told, they simply walked away. But today it is different. It is their first time to be mesmerized by a song. When they reluctantly turn off the audio player, the three Belafonte hits are firmly ensconced in their brains.

When Fatuma reaches home, she takes Ali to the backyard and sings *Day-o* and *Jamaica Farewell* to him. It is the first time his sister has sung anything to him. And she is so joyful. Infected by her spirit, he too sings and croons. *Baba*, who is weeding the *shamba*, looks on in amusement.

After a while, *Mama* gets annoyed.

"What is the matter with you girl, wasting your time. Ali has to take a bath. You have to set the dinner mat and the plates and spoons. *Baba* is about to finish his work. It will be meal time."

Mama serves everyone before she puts food on her plate. Until two years ago, they had eaten in the traditional way, from a single large metal plate. Fatuma had insisted that each person should have his or her own plate. It was good hygiene, she said. *Baba* had agreed but he would have to save the money to buy them. Fatuma had gone ahead, got a loan from Rehema, and purchased an inexpensive used set of four plates and spoons. They looked almost new. At home, she said she had bought the set using the prize money from a science project. Knowing that this girl never says a lie, her parents had accepted her words. She felt guilty about deceiving them, but consoled herself with the thought that it was for a good reason. (She was able to repay the loan after two years when she got the first installment of her university scholarship lodging and meals allowance. By that time, Rehema had forgotten all about it.)

Baba starts the meal with the customary Islamic phrase:

"Bismillah irrahaman irrahim."
(In the name of Allah, most beneficent, most merciful.)

Mama has prepared *matoke*, a plantain dish. As they can rarely afford meat, she has made it with groundnuts and coconut milk. It is her special recipe. All in the family love it. (See the Banana Culture section.)

According to tradition, children eat in silence unless spoken to. *Baba* and *Mama* usually have a day full of stuff to talk about.

But young Ali has become an exception to the rule. A perpetual chatterbox, he has many questions, even at mealtime. And there are unending requests for his parents to buy him a toy, a school item or another thing that has caught his fancy. The elders know that if he is told to behave himself, he will start to cry and not eat his food. So they let him be.

But today it is somewhat different. Today he hums on by himself:

"Six foot, seven foot, eight foot bunch . . . Day-o"

Baba asks:

"What kind of song is that? It sounds strange."

"It is a song about bananas, *Baba*."

Fatuma adds:

"It was the song of banana workers in Jamaica. It helped them bear the pain of their long and difficult work shift."

"Is that so! You should teach it to me, Ali. It will help me too."

At this point, *Mama* loses her temper.

"You crazy girl, one day you will make everyone in this house go mad. Stick to your studies. Do not indulge into the strange habits the youngsters acquire nowadays."

If only *Mama* knew what lay in store for the family.

Day 0821: Interacting with Professor Chachage and their extra readings have affected the outlooks of Fatuma and Rehema in a profound way. Taking keener interest in current affairs, they better grasp what is happening in the nation and the world. They socialize more than before and at times, attend football and basketball matches in the university sports arena.

Yet, their primary focus remains on their areas of specialization, mathematics and physics. Their diligent striving for excellence is noticed by their lecturers right from the first semester. Even though they are first year students, Fatuma is elected the chairperson of the Student Mathematical Society while Rehema leads the Student Physics Club.

One topic where their interests converge is the Theory of Relativity. Formulated by Albert Einstein, it states, among other things, that when an object travels at an extremely high speed, the physical properties we take for granted no longer hold. The passage of time slows down, and the dimensions of the object change. It also postulates that nothing can travel at speeds that are faster than the speed of light, which is about 300,000 kilometers per second. This theory has been verified through many experiments and observations of scientists over the past one hundred years. Yet, since many of its ideas defy common sense, it is not an easy theory to grasp, even for scientists. For example, if you were to travel to a distant star at near the speed of light, upon your return, you would find that your biological age is less than that of your younger sibling.

The girls became attracted to this theory as a result of a course they attended at the end of year one. Rehema finds its cosmological implications fascinating while Fatuma is intrigued by the mathematical techniques it employs. This course was taught by Professor Kessy. While other students were having a hard time, they were able to navigate through its mathematical intricacies and get a reasonable handle on the conceptual basis formulated by Einstein. Many students used to come to them for help. Both of them secured an A+ grade in this course. On top of that, once the course was over, they borrowed advanced books to understand the subject in greater depth. Knowledge, for them, was not just a means to get high grades, but an avenue to expand their mental horizons and better understand the natural and social worlds.

Day 0881: Today, at the start of year two, they enter Professor Kessy's office and respectfully hand him a typed article bearing the title:

A Simpler Conceptualization
of the Special Theory of Relativity.

He keeps them on their feet for thirty minutes as he is absorbed in what he has been given. Looking up, he asks:

"Did you write this?"

"Yes sir, we did."

"Without anyone's help?"

"Yes sir, it is our own work."

"It is truly fantastic; almost unbelievable."

The paper does not contain any new result or report data from an experiment. That much is clear to him. What it provides is a scheme with new types of examples to better understand one of the most complex theories in modern physics. Not only does it indicate the depth of their understanding of this theory but it also represents, in his opinion, a pedagogic milestone.

With their permission, he emails an electronic copy of the paper to the editor of *The Student Journal of Physics* based in the US that afternoon. It is accepted and published four weeks later. It is the first time a paper from East Africa has featured in that prominent journal. Luckily for the girls, the publication is in time for consideration for an annual international prize for a physics paper written by undergraduate students.

Day 0947: The announcement of the winning paper comes two months later. And this year, to the surprise of the international physics fraternity, the winner is a paper written by two students from Africa, Fatuma and Rehema. No student from that part of the world has previously won the prize. Leading American and UK newspapers carry the story, highlighting the fact that it was written by two girls from a low-income nation who essentially did the work on their own. Overnight, they are celebrities, in their own land as well.

Day 0997: It is the day of the prize award ceremony, held in the main assembly hall. The President of the International Union of Physicists has come from New York to do the honors. The Vice Chancellor of the University, the Dean of the Faculty of Science and the Minister of Education are present as well. Fatuma and Rehema shyly ascend the podium. They get a congratulatory handshake from the dignitaries, and are handed the prize plaque and a cash award of five thousand dollars that goes with it.

After the ceremony, a radio reporter asks them:

"How did you manage to do it? Do you have a special method?"

Rehema responds:

"When we work on a problem, we are not discouraged if we do not find the answer immediately. We keep tackling it from different angles."

Fatuma adds:

"And we always work together."

Rehema chimes in:

"We do not eat junk food. Instead of soda and cake, we have water, *karanga* and *ndizi*."

Next day, their smiling faces are splattered across the front pages of the local newspapers. The headlines read:

Our Own Science Geniuses
The Pride of Our Nation
Our Whizz Kids Tame Relativity with Banana

At home, each girl hands over one thousand dollars from the prize money to her ecstatic parents. They set aside a thousand dollars for buying library books and physics lab equipment for their old school. The remaining two thousand dollars are saved in a joint bank account.

Day 1031: On the city streets, in the meantime, an atmosphere of fear has come to prevail. Armed militia patrols in fast jeeps zooming through the city streets are now a routine sight. They run after panicked hawkers and food vendors. The wares of those caught are seized. Some are roughed up. Invariably, they lose a big chunk of their assets and must pay a hefty fine of fifty thousand shillings to be released from custody. The customers are at times embroiled in the melee, or left empty-handed.

The rigmarole never ends. In the case of fruit, vegetable and freshly cooked food sellers, what they sell is essential stuff that is in high demand. But the rigidly minded city authorities make no distinction between them and those who sell shoes, kitchenware, or car window wipers. As the vendors must earn a living, they find creative ways evading the militia, and use cell phones to warn each other. The militia patrols then approach from two or three directions simultaneously. One day chased away, the next, the determined, especially the younger sellers, are back. It is a perpetual cat and mouse game with injurious human consequences.

Day 1033: Today, as is their routine once a week, Fatuma and Rehema go to their favorite *Mama Lishe* for lunch. Together with other food vendors, she sits near a subsidiary campus gate. Students and university workers in good numbers come here for breakfast and midday meal. The food is cheap, fresh and appealing. The girls lust for the *Mama Lishe's* incomparable *ugali* and *kismavu ya nazi*. As they are her regular customers, she greets them with a wide smile. They don't have to say a word; she knows exactly what their order is.

For some unknown reason, perhaps due to its remoteness, this site has not been targeted by the city patrols. But now their luck has run out. Just as they are about to be served, a militia truck materializes, as if from hell. A panic ensues. Their *Mama Lishe* is seized before she can escape. Roughly tossed into the back of the truck, she wails loudly. Her food containers are for the most part emptied onto the pavement. A few are loaded on the truck. Who knows what will be done with them. The customers, angry and hungry, can do nothing but stare in silence.

"What kind of people are these?"

"Where is this world coming to?"

"This is a city for tourists and rich people only."

It is with gnawing tummies and profound sadness that Fatuma and Rehema slowly make their way back to the library.

Day 1049: Their *Mama Lishe* is not seen again. The girls make do with lack luster cafeteria food every day. The incident has jarred their conscience to the bone. A few days later, both join a student human rights group that has been established at the university a year ago: *Voice of the People* (VOP). Its main aim is to protect the rights of the marginalized, vulnerable and downtrodden people in society. Once per month, it holds a public lecture, discussion session or exhibition on a subject that falls within its purview.

Day 1061: Today, VOP has organized a peaceful march from the campus to the mayor's office to complain about the forceful, ongoing harassment of street children, beggars and street sellers by the city militia. The Banana Girls have joined the march.

Rehema carries a placard, which reads:

Banana sellers are not loafers.

Fatuma's placard says:

Our school children have lost 20,000,000 tasty groundnuts.

There are about seventy students present. Each has a placard of his or her own. One says:

We want our Mama Lishe back.

The students chant merrily and walk in tranquility, unaware of the danger ahead. For, just outside the main university gate, a line of city militia guys blocks their way. It is a disturbing sight. And it is a curious standoff. On the one side of the divide is the stern commander, the father, and on the other, a determined daughter. Unbelievingly, he looks at her, and tries to figure out how to rescue her from the fracas about to erupt. Yet, Rehema ignores him; her solidarity lies with her compatriots.

If Mr. Felix had been there, he would have wondered:

"What is the probability of such a father-daughter encounter? One in a million, or one in a hundred million?"

The girls have another computation swirling in their heads:

"What is the chance that one day *Baba* Fatuma, *Mzee* Salum, *Mama Lishe* and other food vendors be allowed again to ply in peace and offer their healthy, hearty products to the residents of this beautiful city?"

"Or is it a hopeless struggle?"

When they find their march blocked, the protestors decide to sit down on the tarmac, and continue to chant, louder than before. In the spirit of the civil rights struggles of 1960s in the US, they sing: "*We shall overcome, some day …*" A crowd of onlookers stands at a distance. *Baba* Rehema barks a command and his *askaris* swoop down on the students. None of them resists. Each is picked up, one by one, and haughtily pushed onto the awaiting trucks.

At the police station, they are fingerprinted, photographed and interrogated.

"Who has incited you?"

"Who is paying you?"

"Are you a member of the opposition party?"

"Don't you know what you are doing is illegal?"

"Have you joined the university to study or make trouble?"

The students respond uniformly, indicating that they decided to march on their own, in a peaceful manner to exercise their right to express their views, as permitted by the Constitution of the nation. Despite the threatening tone of the interrogators, and extensive questioning, they do not alter what they say.

It is late in the afternoon when Rehema and Fatuma come to their homes to be hugged and bugged by their anxious *mamas*. Because of *Baba* Rehema's influence, they were released but with a stern warning not to repeat their misdeeds. Fatuma is nursing a painful shoulder she acquired upon being pushed into the militia van. Though miles apart, both get the same lecture, and at the same time.

"First you talk weird things. And now this. When are you going to grow up? Soon you have to marry, raise children. Who will accept you if you have such outlandish habits?"

Both hug their *mamas* and wipe the tears off their faces.

"It is OK, *Mama*, it is OK. We are doing fine."

Mr. Marufu, had he been able to observe what was happening at these homes would have been deeply worried:

"Where are my gentle, smart students headed?"

The identical nature of what was happening at both the places would have bugged him to no end.

"Is it a case of telepathy?"

Yet, it is a convention bound society. What mothers expect from their daughters is fairly uniform. The identical nature of the two mother-daughter interactions is quite predictable.

What no one suspects is that the girls want to turn conventional wisdom upside down. It is as if the spirit of the sixties is resurrecting itself. Not content with trifles, their motto in life now is:

Be a Realist
Demand the Impossible

Day 1171: The day they had fervently dreamed about is here at last. After the second year exams, the Banana Girls have six weeks of teaching practice. They had lobbied to be assigned to the same school. Not only was their request granted but also that school is none other than their old high school.

Today they begin the teaching practice. They are up early and put on attires that are quite alike: a laced white blouse upon a pleated gray skirt. From the prize money, *Mama* Fatuma had bought three dresses for her daughter, her first time to make a costly purchase. When Rehema saw them, she had her *Mama* buy identical dresses for herself from the same shop.

Both arrive at the school, by *daladala*, well before assembly time and report at Mr. Marufu's office. They are expected. Mr. Felix, who will be their local supervisor, is also there.

They are greeted with warmth and joy. As the girls have looked at the syllabus and prepared their initial series of lessons, they can begin right away. Fatuma will teach mathematics to Form IA. Her plan is to start with a topic in algebra, simultaneous equations in two unknowns, and introduce it in practice terms. She will use the example about buying fruits from the market once used by Mr. Felix.

Banana Problem 3

Asha buys 3 bananas and 4 mangoes for 2,900 shillings; Alice buys 4 bananas and 3 mangoes for 2,100 shillings. Janet has to buy 5 bananas and 5 mangoes. How much money does she need?

Rehema will teach physics to Form IB. Starting with the topics of heat and temperature, she will do an experiment to convert water from solid to liquid to gas to illustrate these basic ideas.

The girls are nervous at the outset. Mr. Marufu and Mr. Felix know that they will put in their best efforts and become competent teachers in no time. Mr. Felix advises:

"The essential things are that you understand your subject and have the interests of your students at heart. That will make you confident and effective teachers in no time."

And it did work out well. When their university supervisor came to the school two weeks later, he was highly impressed at their classroom performance and the manner in which their students responded to them.

There was one critical matter over which their former teachers were initially apprehensive. They had heard about the activism of their star students and the trouble they had landed into. They hoped that these unpredictable youngsters would not engage in similar activities or negatively influence the students here.

Happily for the headmaster, the girls confine themselves to class work. When they take students out for practical tasks, it is related to the topic being covered in class.

Day 1193: There is one extracurricular activity they seek to undertake. It is to organize a joint competition to memorize the digits of the mathematical constant π for their students. Mr. Marufu readily grants the request; Mr. Felix is in favor of it too.

The two trainee teachers hand out a sheet of paper with the first one thousand digits of Pi (π = 3.14159265358979323...., the full list is in the Banana Mathematics section) and challenge their students to commit to memory as many digits as they can. An open oral test will be held after three weeks. To qualify for the final round, memorization of the first fifteen digits is required. The top two performers in the final round will each get a book prize.

Day 1213: It is the Pi competition day. Four boys and six girls from the two classes have attained the qualifying level. Mr. Marufu wants the final competition to take place in the main hall in front of the entire school.

The winners are Samya at 37 digits and Sylvester at 29 digits. Each gets a copy *The Joy of Pi* by David Blatner from the headmaster. It is a short, non-technical book on the history and computation of π. After thunderous applause for the winners from the audience, Mr. Marufu expresses thanks to Fatuma and Rehema for organizing the event and donating the books. He says it should inspire all present, and that the school will make it an annual event.

Mr. Felix has a question for Fatuma and Rehema. As he has asked it earlier, he knows the answer. But he wants a public response:

"How many digits of π have you memorized?"

Instead of giving a number, first Rehema takes the stage. She errs at the 54th digit; her score is 53 digits. Fatuma nearly doubles it by stopping at 97 digits.

Everyone stands up and claps on for almost five minutes. How do they manage it? People wonder.

Rehema explains:

"Our scores actually are not extraordinary. The world record for memorizing the digits of π is held by Suresh K Sharma of India. In October 2015, he correctly recited 70,030 digits in 17 hours and 14 minutes. The second place is held by a fellow Indian, Rajveer Meena, who six months earlier had got 70,000 digits correct."

The audience is dumbstruck at such unbelievable achievements. Fatuma adds:

"Do not think that it is a question of innate ability or biological superiority. Until the year 1979, the field of π memorization was dominated by Europeans and North Americans. However, all the world record holders since then have emerged from Asia. Of the ten highest records, the first eight are from India, Japan or China, and the last two from Europe. The highest European performance thus far stands at 22,612 digits."

Mr. Marufu asks the question that is on many minds:

"What about Africa?"

Rehema responds:

"Unfortunately, we are lagging far behind. Our highest score, set in South Africa in 2016, is 661 digits. It is followed by 365 digits from Nigeria. The highest East African achievement is 50 digits, from Kenya in 2012."

Both the girls have surpassed the East African mark. But since it was not achieved under internationally accepted rules, it does not count. Fatuma elaborates:

"Digit memorization is a matter of practice, technique and determination. There are special methods you can use to remember large amount of information. These are explained on many websites and books. The fact that one of you memorized 37 digits within three weeks without any help shows that the potential for high scores exists."

And, finally, Fatuma adds her few words of wisdom:

"The main problem is with the system of education. It needs to place equal weight on memorizing facts using good methods and developing an understanding of facts with the help of ideas and theories. At the moment, it focuses on rote memorization, just for passing an examination. As soon as the exam is over, all is forgotten."

One student has a question:

"Is not π digit memorization also rote memorization?"

"Memorizing the digits of π is internationally regarded as the ultimate mental marathon. But, as in a marathon race, it is not just a question of innate ability and stamina. A marathon runner must have an effective strategy, ensure adequate water and glucose intake, pace herself appropriately, coordinate with team mates and prepare herself psychologically. To complete a mental marathon also requires strategy, planning and effective techniques. Before books were in wide use, our ancestors were using such methods to remember large amounts of information which was passed down orally from generation to generation. We have forgotten them. The modern memory-saving devices we use, like cell phones, make the situation worse."

She continues:

"We need to balance memorization and understanding of ideas, and use good memorization techniques."

Mr. Marufu reflects to himself:

"What fine words of wisdom! I wish officials from the Ministry of Education were here."

Day 1229: Before the final week of teaching practice, the girls hand over 800 dollars of their prize money to Mr. Marufu. It is for books and laboratory supplies. They also donate books worth 200 dollars for the school library. The gifts are accepted with gratitude.

At break time, they give a shirt and a pair of pants to *Mzee* Simon, the maintenance worker. He is overcome with tears of joy.

Day 1237: Today, their teaching practice ends. It has been a successful and happy six weeks for them, their students and the school.

During school assembly, three of their students recite a poem in their honor. First they say it in Swahili and then in English:

Teacher, teacher	*Mwalimu, mwalimu*
Our beloved teachers	*Walimu wapenzi*
With math and physics	*Hisabati na fisikia*
We got fun and laughter	*Yalileta kichekesho pia*
Reflection and analysis	*Fikra na uchambuzi*
And good work habits	*Na tabia njema*
Though we are sad	*Tumekosa furaha lakini*
We wish you the best	*Tunawatakieni kilalaheri*
We shall remember you	*Tutawakumbukeni*
We shall remember you	*Tutawakumbukeni*
Teacher, teacher	*Mwalimu, mwalimu*

LIBERATION

Day 1249: All science finalists undertake a research project. With a month of vacation time left, Fatuma and Rehema make an early start. They team up with Alice, a smart chemistry major, for a joint project. The project work is usually done on an individual basis. But, given the nature of what they want to do, and the good reputation they have with the academic staff, their request for collaborative research is granted. Their topic is:

A Preliminary Investigation into the
Production of Banana Paper

The bark and stem of the banana plant and the peel are used in several Asian countries to produce paper. These girls want to examine the scientific basis of the manufacturing process so as to lay a foundation for a full-scale feasibility study in the future. Their project incorporates challenging chemistry, physics and math related components, thus fulfilling the requirements of each of their departments. It also has a potential for practical application.

It is vacation time. There is hardly anyone around. The trio are, unbeknownst to their supervisors, also doing experiments of a different type in the chemistry lab. But they do not mention it to anyone.

Alice is the daughter of a prosperous businessman who owns a road transport company that ferries goods to upcountry regions and neighboring countries. His fleet operates from a gigantic depot located at the outskirts of the city. It has nearly a hundred container-carrying trucks. Her elder brother Jonathan manages the fleet. In addition, *Baba* Alice has three motor vehicle spare parts shops in different parts of the city.

They live in a spacious mansion half a kilometer from the university that boasts a large garden dotted with multicolored flowering plants and a fountain in the middle. A team of ten uniformed house servants maintains the place. Alice comes to the university in a chauffeur-driven car.

Like the Banana Girls, Alice has both a passion for excellence in science and a sense of dedication to social justice. They had met at a meeting of *Voice of the People*, and subsequently had bonded well.

Day 1277: Alice has taken Fatuma and Rehema to her place for lunch. Both are literally blown away by what they see: the fancy chandeliers on the ceiling, the immaculate furniture, the three giant sized refrigerators in the kitchen and the 48-inch TV screen. At lunch, they feel they are attending a king's feast; the only missing item was bananas. When Fatuma narrates her experience to her family later in the evening, they think she is making it up.

Day 1279: They are on an extended lunch break in the campus cafeteria. It was a tiring morning but they are in a good mood. After days of trial and error, their experiment has begun to yield positive results.

Rehema poses a frank query to Alice:

"You are from a very rich family. How come you are concerned about poor people?"

Alice has a clear answer:

"It started when I was in primary school. *Baba* was always busy with his business. *Mama* was engrossed with her friends. I was looked after by *Bibi* Aisha. She served me my meals, gave me bath, dressed me for school and church, arranged my toys and played with me. Her stories and the traditional songs she sang at bedtime were so enchanting. I loved her; she was a second mother to me."

"But she was not treated well. *Mama* shouted at her and gave her leftover food. She became so unhappy but she always was kind and gentle with me."

"I really wanted to see where she lived. There was a time when *Mama* was on a trip and *Baba* was engrossed in work. She took me on a bus to her place. It was just a single room; the shared toilet had cockroaches and stank like anything. I almost threw up. But her cheerful demeanor, hot *chai* and sweet *mandazi* made me ignore everything."

After a pause, she continues:

"One day, when I had just started secondary school, *Mama* accused her of breaking a glass plate. It was not true; someone else had done it. *Bibi* Aisha denied the charge. *Mama* told her that her that not only was she careless but also insolent. "From tomorrow, you do not have to come to work.""

"That was it. In an instant, she vanished from my life. That night and for many nights, I cried myself to sleep. But I never forgot her. One weekend, when I was in Form V, I secretly went to her place. I still remembered where it was. She was overjoyed. At first, she thought it was a dream. She had aged a lot. Walking was painful and difficult. Her eyesight was fading. She was told at the district health center that she had diabetes but had no money for medicine."

Again, Alice pauses; clearly, it is an emotional topic for her.

"Since then, I have been visiting her about once a month. I give her money for food and health expenses. She feels better now. When I am busy with course work, our driver takes the money to her. He is the only person who knows my secret. He and *Bibi* Aisha had started work at our place almost at the same time, and know each other well. Of late, he has become apprehensive. He is getting on in age, and fears that soon he will be replaced by a young fellow."

Again a pause:

"I am sorry. It is not easy for me to say this. You are the first people to whom I am pouring out what has been buried in my heart."

"That is OK, Alice. Take it easy. We are completely with you."

"You see, visiting *Bibi* Aisha has shown me things I never knew existed. I had lived a totally isolated life. Now I know that there are thousands of elderly people living like her in our city. And there are even more children who are hungry and sick. How can I close my eyes and forget that? How?"

"I want to live a simple life and help the poor. *Mama* gives me jewelry and expensive watches. I do not wear them. She mocks me saying that no boy will be attracted to a plain girl like me. I do not care. I want to be a scientist."

"This girl truly has a heart of gold." So think Fatuma and Rehema.

Under their influence, Alice too is in no time smitten by the banana. The three often sit together at lunch. A keen observer would deduce that the membership of the august "Banana Fan Club" has increased by fifty percent!

Day 1283: At lunchtime, Alice seems excited, eager to tell them something:

"I had an interesting interaction with my brother yesterday."

"Tell us about it."

"He called for me the moment I reached home. He was sitting in the balcony with his girlfriend. I like her. I don't know how she can stand him – he is so money-minded."

"Sis, what is this?" He was referring to the bottle in his hand.

"Beer, of course." Because that is what he always has.

"Aha, but it is special beer."

Though it was a bottle of a kind I had not seen, I just said, "I see nothing special about it."

"You like bananas, don't you?"

"And what of it?"

"Well, this is banana beer, in fact, the best of the lot."

"Though I dislike beer, he persuaded me to take two sips. It had a banana-ish flavor but it was not to my taste. He then gave me a long lecture on beer and money."

"I will tell you the main points. The banana beer is produced by a local brewery, yet, it is among the most expensive beers here. In the supermarket, a bottle is 6,000 shillings and in a hotel, it is 7,000 shillings."

"Wow, that is more money than my *Baba* earns in a day!" Fatuma exclaims.

"The company that owns the brewery has a stock market value of 50 million US dollars. A foreign investor owns four fifths of the stock. He wants to raise capital to expand production. You see, though it is costly, its popularity among the tourists and the moneyed people is rising. The export demand is also high. The investor has put a fourth of his company shares for public auction."

"That is where my brother comes in. He told me he bought shares worth 10,000 US dollars yesterday morning. He told me, "Sis, you should encourage your friends to drink this beer. The more it is sold, the more cash in our pockets.""

"When I said they would not be able to afford it, he replied, "First you buy it for them and when they get hooked, they will do it on their own." I don't know if he was joking or not, but that was my introduction to the fancy banana beer."

Fatuma has her own story to add:

"Many years ago, my *Baba* used to make and sell banana beer. I remember he had so many customers. He doesn't do it anymore because it was banned by the city council. Isn't it ironic, he has been deprived of a good source of income and his customers cannot have their favorite drink but the foreign investor makes plenty of money by selling it to those who can afford his luxury product."

Alice wonders:

"Maybe what your *Baba* was producing was not that hygienic."

"That is what they said. Yet it has been a traditional drink for our community for at least a hundred years. I do not recall my *Baba*'s customers complaining or getting sick."

Rehema has a suggestion that seems quite reasonable:

"Instead of banning the product, they could have formed groups of traditional brewers into cooperatives and given them loans to set up small-scale industries and trained them in making and bottling the beer under hygienic conditions. Today, there would have been a good supply of affordable banana beer for the local market. And income for your *Baba* too."

Alice concurs:

"That is exactly what they should have done. In our home area people have been brewing plantains with millet flour to make a delightful drink called *mbege*. It has been so popular, a must at weddings and major occasions. Nowadays, however, more and more people prefer factory made drinks. It is said to be a sign of modernity."

Fatuma adds in a despondent tone:

"I am sure the fancy banana beer costs much less to produce. The investor is taking advantage of the craze for exotic things among the foreigners and the wealthy. Like the others, he must be giving lousy pay to the factory floor workers. With his daily wage, the worker cannot buy anything more than a single bottle of the beer he makes. The investor will send the super profits he makes to his home country. How do our people benefit? I do not know why our government cannot have better policies for our nation."

Rehema has the final word:

"Whatever the politicians proclaim, it is the investors who are running the show."

That evening, Fatuma had a long talk with her *Baba* about the beer he used to brew. He was happy to answer her queries.

"My daughter, what I was making was not *Mbege*. I was using sweet bananas. My father had showed me how to make it."

He explained to her the intricate process for making banana beer.

"It needs a lot of practice before you can have something people will like. I was persistent and became good at it. People in the neighborhood, and even those from afar would flock to get it."

Baba wished he could restart that business. His big regret was that his skill would disappear with him.

Day 1289: They have come to seek advice from Professor Chachage.

"Professor, everyone says that science and politics do not mix, that sooner or later, we will have to choose, either this or that. What is your view?"

"Well, I think it is simple minded to call your activities outside the classroom 'politics.' You are expressing concern for your fellow human beings. That is what all students should do. The problem is not with you but with the majority who are too self-centered to care."

The girls find these words most assuring. He adds:

"And you do not have to make a choice. Albert Einstein was an activist for global peace, nuclear disarmament and civil rights. He was also a socialist and wrote a famous essay entitled "*Why Socialism?*" for the inaugural issue of the *Monthly Review* magazine. Bertrand Russell, a preeminent mathematician and logician of the 20th century, was an outspoken pacifist and campaigner for human rights. And there are many more examples. Do not get distracted by what others tell you. Let me show you a relevant quote."

He locates it on his computer and prints it out.

Only a life lived for others is worth living.

Albert Einstein

"You are in fine company. You go where your heart and mind direct you."

They leave his office in a distinctly buoyant mood.

Day 1301: The academic year is in full swing. The final year courses are more demanding. In order to cope, Fatuma stays in a student dorm. The three girls have a major advantage over the other students: while most are just formulating their project topic, the girls have already put finishing touches to the Banana Paper project.

Day 1303: In the meantime, scandals are afoot in the city. For a few weeks, the papers have been abuzz with stories about a financial collusion of dubious legality between Mr. JP Mrema, a prominent contractor, and Mr. W Nsekela, the Deputy Mayor. Up to a hundred million shillings is said to have surreptitiously changed hands in connection with a massive public transport construction project. The police spokesman says no evidence of wrongdoing has been found. But the public feels that a thorough investigation has not been undertaken.

Day 1361: The newspaper headlines today are unparalleled. As Mr. Mrema and Mr. Nsekela were being driven to work yesterday, their fancy saloons suddenly grinded to a halt. Smoke with a strange odor oozed from the engine. The same thing happened later to six other automobiles they own. Foul play is suspected. The mechanics are puzzled. They think some liquid was poured into the petrol tanks, leading to overheating and a brown out in the engine.

Day 1381: The newspapers blare with hysteria. The vehicles of the Mayor, the Minister of Transport and the businesswoman who runs the firm that will supply construction material for the mammoth transport project fall prey to the same treatment. All their vehicles slowly come to an immovable stop in traffic; the cause is the same; but how the deed was done, and by whom remains a mystery.

There is but a faint clue. Printed leaflets plastered on the walls of a few buildings bear an identical sentence:

THE CROOKS DESERVED WHAT THEY GOT. BLF

Who are the *BLF*? It is the talk of the town. The popular view is, whoever they are, all power to them. The shameless crooks got what they deserved.

Day 1399: The antics of the *BLF* continue. The targets vary. A corrupt official, or manager of a local or foreign company that hikes up the prices of basic goods, creates artificial shortages, or pays miserable wages to workers is struck. It has created a climate of fear among the big shots in the nation. They can stand arrests by the police. But becoming a public spectacle – that they truly loathe. With their power, financial might and high priced lawyers, they usually wriggle out of the former. Shaming in front of the entire nation, that is quite another thing. It turns them into a perpetual laughing stock.

Today, it is the senior official of a bank that charges exorbitant interest to rural farmers who has been put to shame. Leaflets are seen once again but with a difference. They say:

We Stand for Accountability,
Social Justice and Economic Fairness. BLF

It clarifies the motivations of the perpetrators, yet deepens the mystery as to their identity. Who can these *BLF* people be? Nobody, including the police, can figure it out. Their popularity rises.

Day 1409: The state officials are highly alarmed. Key organs of society are being undermined. A cabinet meeting resolves that drastic measures are needed to contain this emergent threat to civic order. A foreign terrorist group or hostile nation is possibly orchestrating the attacks. The *BLF* has not engaged in violent acts, or harmed any person. Nevertheless a presidential decree declares it a terrorist organization. According to law, this makes membership in the group punishable by a minimum sentence of twenty years in prison.

Day 1423: The word "terrorism" carries global connotations. It immediately draws the attention of the American government. Upon instruction from Washington, its ambassador pledges full support in combatting the new menace. As it is an anticipated offer, it is readily accepted. The US Secretary of State makes a personal phone call to the Minister for Foreign Affairs giving the details of funds, counter-terrorism officers, technical equipment and intelligence support that will be provided. A ten-member team from the Center for Global Terrorism Control flies over the same week and starts implementing a three-pronged strategy (sophisticated surveillance and decoding devices, enhanced interrogation techniques and refined perception management) to identify and defeat this terrorist group. Gradually, the tables begin to turn against the *BLF.*

Day 1427: Petrol samples from the affected vehicles are sent to a special lab in the US. Surprisingly, it is discovered that a small amount of ripe banana dissolved in an organic solvent was added into the petrol tank, forming a mixture with chemical properties designed to damage the engine of an automobile.

Only a person with a good knowledge of chemistry and access to the right kind of raw materials and equipment could have created it. Electronic surveillance of city-wide cell phone traffic and other investigations point towards the university chemistry lab, and a third year student, Alice, who has been working on a project related to bananas.

Day 1429: In the evening, Alice waits for her driver to take her home. Just then, a car with darkened windows pulls up. Two muscular men come out, and before she can react in any way, they grab her and put her onto the back seat. Within a minute, the car speeds away. At ten o'clock, her frantic father makes a missing person report to the police. As he is a major donor to the ruling party, a citywide search is mounted within the hour. But there is no sign of the young girl. The police feel that she has been kidnapped for ransom or revenge. It makes headlines the next day.

The papers quote a police spokesman that no clues have emerged thus far.

In fact, Alice is in a secret state detention facility. She is placed in a tiny high-walled cell with a toilet, and a small window ten feet above the floor. There is nothing else. For the first five days, she encounters total silence. A meal plate slipped twice a day via an opening in the door has half cooked gruel with a few boiled beans. For the next five days, loud music is played near the door for twenty-four hours a day. The meals are the same. She cannot sleep and has no human contact.

Day 1439: When the cell door is opened on the eleventh day, a smelly, emaciated figure lies on the ground. Alice has been deprived of her dignity and humanity.

Suffering from extreme mental and physical exhaustion, Alice is unable to resist her interrogators and reveals everything. *BLF*, she tells them, stands for *Banana Liberation Front*. It has fifty members, all young girls between the ages of 18 and 25. About half are university students; the rest work in different jobs. They are from varied social strata -- wealthy merchants, senior state officials, professionals as well as low paid workers and street vendors. The group was founded and is led by Rehema and Fatuma, two final year students at the university.

Armed with this information, the authorities know that the days of *BLF* are numbered. The American specialists advise them not to move on the group immediately. First, an appropriate psychological mood has to be created, otherwise the arrests may backfire in political terms.

Alice is fed and treated well. No overt sign of her ordeal remains.

Day 1451: The newspapers of the day are gripped by strange headlines. In the main, they proclaim:

Bananas pose a threat to
human physical and mental health.

They derive from a study recently completed by two professors of public health at the university. They used a sample of two-thousand people afflicted with five categories of health and behavioral problems. Their findings are:

1. 83% of people with newly diagnosed diabetes had previously eaten more than 10 bananas a week.
2. 95% of people with cancer are lifetime consumers of bananas.
3. 91% of school children with major discipline issues are addicted to bananas.
4. 90% of schizophrenics can consume seven or more bananas at a time.
5. 88% of people who are late to work often crave for bananas.

The professors have a long record of scientific publications in reputed journals. They declare that their results are statistically significant, precise and of high external validity. The journalists do not know what this means. But it sounds impressive, and so it is repeated in the print and broadcast media stories.

Their study is given greater credibility by the fact that earlier in the year, the US Embassy had honored these professors with the Annual Martin Luther King Award in recognition of their exemplary record of civic engagement and contribution to public health.

But why overconsumption of bananas has such toxic effects has yet to be ascertained. Another scientist points to the high potassium level of the fruit, noting that a part of it is radioactive. Eating bananas in excess may deposit the radioactive atoms of the mineral in a specific area of the brain and interfere with the functioning of vital body organs. That is his claim.

The expressed consensus is that banana consumption must be controlled, especially among children. Else it can be as harmful to human health as cigarettes. The media loudly and repeatedly echo these views.

Day 1453: However, a number of experts do not accept them. One radio station airs the views of two skeptical professors. But as the interview is being broadcast, the Mayor enters the studio with armed militiamen and shuts it down on the ground that it is providing support to terrorists. Everyone present is issued a stern warning.

The next day newspaper editorials voice strong complaints. One editorial says:

> The action by the Mayor to shut down a live broadcast has shocked us. It was a legitimate program discussing the scientific merits of a health study. He said it had to stop because it was "promoting terrorism." When asked what talking about bananas and health has to do with terrorism, he said, "You will soon find out."
>
> Our Honorable Mayor has given a new meaning to the legal principle "Ignorance of the law excuses no one." Now you can be charged with an offense even if the fact that the act in question is illegal has been kept a state secret. And the Mayor had no court order or an authorization from the Minister for Information, as is required by law.

Despite these grave concerns, no action is taken by the higher authorities. The upshot of it is that from then on, all media keep silent on the issue, fearing that otherwise they may be branded as sympathizers or worse of terrorism.

Day 1459: The stage is almost set. The Ministry of Health has publicized the findings of the banana health study through radio announcements and flyers distributed in schools and public places. The public mood is turning anti-banana. Some mothers do not give bananas to their kids anymore.

Day 1471: The Anti-terrorism Squad determines that it is the right time to nab the members of the *BLF*. Guided by electronic surveillance, contingents in full body armor swoop down on all its fifty members, including the two leaders. It is a citywide operation. In homes, work places and the university, they take into custody young girls calmly going about their ordinary lives. Journalists and TV reporters are taken along to witness the arrest. At the same time, Alice is given an unpublicized reprieve and sent home for having cooperated with the authorities. That her father is a well-connected businessman also played a role in this decision.

The newspaper headlines tell it all:

Anarchist gang smashed.
Banana crazed terrorists arrested.
The BLF is no more.

The Mayor issues a statement:

> A group of young girls were driven to insane political extremism by overindulgence in bananas. Led by two brilliant but fanatic university students, their organization was bent on creating havoc and destroying the fabric of society. They are as dangerous as the extremists who plant bombs. It is likely that they had support from a foreign entity. I thank the American government for providing timely help in our crusade against terrorism.

People are flabbergasted when the names of the members and leaders of the *BLF* are made public.

> "At home, in school and work, they are so well behaved."

> "You cannot trust anyone these days."

> "Bananas are truly dangerous. They can make a decent person mad."

In early times it was about pot. But now the government may issue a different warning, especially to the youth:

> Do not consume more than one banana a day.
> The excess Vitamin B6 and Potassium can induce
> hallucinations.

Day 1481: Ever since the arrest of Rehema and Fatuma, there is a changed atmosphere in their homes. *Baba* Rehema is intensely frustrated by what he experiences at work. Behind his back, his junior and senior colleagues appear to be saying:

> "You are a militia commander but your daughter has become a terrorist. How could you not bring her up to be a law-abiding citizen? You have failed to fulfill your responsibility as a parent."

People shun his company. Important assignments that earlier came to him are now channeled to others. He resorts to alcohol in greater quantity, coming home late at night in drunken stupor and screams at his wife.

At Fatuma's place, a sad silence prevails. Even the ebullient Ali is subdued. He asks the same questions, over and over:

> "Where is my *dada*? When is she coming home?"

His parents have no answer, but pray for their beloved girl. The neighbors do not visit anymore. The banana merchant has abandoned them too. It is only through the generosity of *Baba's* brother that the family can keep going.

Alice is aware of the challenges faced by Fatuma's family. But she is forbidden to go outside the mansion gate. With the help of her driver, she manages to send a good sum of money to them. It will be used to buy school supplies for Ali.

Day 1483: Palpable tension pervades the city. From early hours, armed police patrols are roaming the streets. The main courtroom is surrounded by a military contingent. The trial of the leaders of the *BLF* is to start.

The courtroom overflows with spectators and media. Fatuma and Rehema's parents, unable to go inside, stand near the door. They can barely hear what is going on inside. Journalists mulling around bombard them with questions upon questions. They have nothing to say. The mothers only shed tears.

The case is being heard before Judge Wilma Shirima. The prosecution would have preferred someone else. But it can live with her since, if the evidence is beyond doubt, she tends to impose the maximal penalty allowed under the law. On the other hand, the defense knows that she is fair and open-minded, and, at times, can reach a verdict that goes against the grain. In contrast to many jurists currently on the bench, she is not one to be influenced by political authority. Her grasp of the fine points of the principles of jurisprudence, existent laws and precedent-setting cases is said to be encyclopedic. That a decision reached by her is overturned upon appeal is an almost unheard of event. Hence, because of its possible international ramifications, the Chief Justice has selected a judge with such an impeccable reputation to oversee this trial.

The state attorney presents his case. He was counting on Alice to testify against her compatriots. But she backed down at the last minute. The main evidence he presents are the intercepted communications, high resolution satellite images, the results of the banana study and the history of activism of the accused. It looks like an air-tight case.

Fatuma and Rehema are represented by a lawyer from a local human rights group, Ms Leticia Lissu. She, however, lacks the experience to mount a solid defense. Fortunately, Professor

Chachage and Professor Issa from the School of Law are on hand to provide substantive and legal support. She advises her clients to plead not guilty by reasons of insanity; that eating bananas in excess had made them unable to distinguish right from wrong and loose control over their actions. But the girls reject that line of defense. Their lawyer now plans to rely on mitigating arguments like young age, generally good behavior and lack of prior convictions to persuade the judge to give them a light sentence.

In the afternoon, one of the professors who led the banana and health study gives his expert testimony. At one point, the girls raise their hands. Their lawyer tells them in a hushed tone that it is not allowed. A court officer comes to say the same thing. But the hands remain up. The judge looks at them sharply. For five minutes, she ignores them. Then she relents:

> "This is highly unusual, young ladies. But given the serious charges you face, and if your counsel has no objection, I will allow it. Do you have a question for the witness?"

> "Yes, your honor."

> "Well, well, I do not see what harm it can do. I will allow each of you to ask a short question."

The state attorney, while distinctly unhappy, is reluctant to contradict the judge unless he has a strong standing in rule and law. He has realized that Judge Shirima, like most people in the room, must be wondering how the young, skinny, naïve-looking girls could be classified as terrorists. From the start of the trial, she has displayed a sympathetic demeanor towards them. When Ms Lissu had petitioned the court to remove the heavily-armed police from the courtroom and take the cuffs from the hands of her clients on the grounds that (a) presently they posed no threat to anyone and (b) these things created a prejudicial atmosphere in the courtroom, the judge had accepted the petition.

Fatuma asks the professor:

1. What is the percentage of people who do not have cancer who are lifetime fans of bananas?

2. What is the percentage of people who come to work on time who also crave bananas?

Rehema asks:

"One of your colleagues earlier did a child welfare study which showed that nearly seventy percent of the nation's children live in poverty and continually face the perils of ill health. Is that in any way connected to the consumption or non-consumption of bananas?"

The professor is perplexed. But before he can reply, the state attorney intervenes.

"Your honor, I object in the strongest terms. The questions are irrelevant and inappropriate, and will only divert our attention to issues that are beyond the purview of this case. We are not concerned about those who are healthy and well behaved but those who are not. They attack the credibility of our witness, who with his colleague, is among the top health experts in this nation. The two have received international scientific honors. Most of the questions posed by the defendants are based on speculation, not scientific data. I request your honor to disallow them. As the court procedure requires, all questions to the witness must be channeled through their legal counsel."

The judge ponders for a while, and then declares:

"You points are valid in law and fact. I order the defendants to restrain themselves. The questions are withdrawn. You may proceed with your case."

The next day the prosecutor presents the final piece of evidence against the girls. He claims that they had external help that was used to fund their criminal activities and devise the elaborate code they had used for communication.

Ms Lissu counters the first claim with a bank statement for a joint account the girls had established with their science prize money. The withdrawal pattern indicates that the activities of the *BLF* were likely funded through this account.

The secret code entered into evidence by the prosecutor has three operational stages based on two sets of numbers. Set A is a list of the first thirty-one prime numbers:

$$A = \{2,3,5,7,11,13,17,19,23, \ldots 109,113,127\}$$

If you want to send a coded message on the seventh day of the month, you select the seventh number in this list. This is 17.

List B has the first 1,000 digits of the mathematical constant π, which, however, are placed in a reverse order. It starts with the 1,000th digit, then the 999th digit, then the 998th digit and so on until you reach the second and first digit. (The first 1,000 digits of π are shown in the Banana Mathematics section). To write a message on the selected day, you skip the first 17 digits in List B. From this point on you demarcate the rest of the digits into consecutive groups of five. Of these, the first 26 groups stand for the 26 letters of the alphabet, and the next ten groups for the numerals 0 to 9. A few of the remaining groups denote basic symbols like , . + - etc. and blank space. This scheme was allegedly used by the *BLF* to send a short message of the day in the form of numbers. The recipient would separate the numbers into groups of five and decode the message.

BLF was organized in seven cells with seven members per cell. Fatuma was the overall leader. Alice was a cell leader, and was also in charge of communication. She sent coded messages to the other cell leaders, who would then inform the cell members in person. All messages were in Swahili.

This scheme had been uncovered from the intercepts done by the American National Security Agency. Despite having the most powerful supercomputer in the world at their disposal, it had taken the Agency's top cipher development experts almost a week to determine the nature of the coding scheme.

The prosecutor claims that this level of sophistication was a clear indicator of external assistance. To counter it, the defense counsel calls Professor Kessy. He informs the court that the two girls had sufficient expertize in mathematics to devise on their own not only this code but an even more intricate one.

Day 1487: Nevertheless, the outcome of the trial is predictable. Within three days, it is over. The two girls are found guilty as charged.

Day 1489: During the sentencing phase, Ms Lissu first calls their former schoolteachers and university lecturers to give evidence of the generally good character and behavior of the defendants. They are followed by Professor Chachage, who is asked to provide the global context for the term "banana terrorism."

The prosecutor objects:

> "Your honor, we do not need an academic lecture. We must focus only on fact and law."

The judge asks Ms Lissu to explain the relevance of the professor's testimony.

> "Your honor, the defendants have been branded as "terrorists". But today it has become an emotive label that is frequently used for political propaganda. The professor's testimony will give the court a factual and historical context. It will assist the court to view the defendants' actions in perspective."

> "That sounds reasonable. You may proceed."

Professor Chachage describes the sordid history of the global banana trade and the actions of the American corporations and governmental agencies that overthrew democratically elected leaders, supported brutal dictators and harmed the limbs and lives of tens of thousands ordinary human beings.

Upon hearing that, the judge inquires:

"How do we know that what you are saying is true? For all we know, it may be political propaganda."

The professor explains how this history has been documented by human rights organizations, respected investigators and journalists from the US and elsewhere, as well as in scores of parliamentary and legal proceedings. To back up his words, he introduces five books into evidence.

"Your honor, here is a newspaper report from the US that says that in 2007, the US Department of Justice imposed a fine of 25 million dollars on the world's largest banana company, Chiquita Bananas. This was done because the company had provided funds to a known terrorist organization in Colombia. These companies are also facing court cases for human rights violations and use of dangerous chemicals without regard to the health of the plantation workers."

At the end of the professor's presentation, Ms Lissu draws a potent conclusion:

"Your honor, despite the clear evidence that these companies, their officials, their government and its officers have engaged in such illegal acts of violence, none are labeled as terrorists or terroristic entities. Only rarely is a fine imposed but no one is sent to prison. But these two girls and their group, whose actions have not caused physical harm to any person, have, in law and general parlance, been reflexively labeled as terrorists. Is that just and fair?"

The judge is informed, impressed, shocked and disturbed by what she has heard. She spends the night reading one of the books submitted by Professor Chachage, reviewing the case law and evidence, and formulating her ruling.

Even for the learned jurist, it is an eye-opening night. She is deeply shocked when she reads about the Banana Massacre that occurred in Colombia in December 1928. Two thousand or so striking but unarmed workers on a banana plantation owned by the Boston-based United Fruit were gunned down in cold blood for demanding their basic rights. Their family members were also killed. The US representative reported the event to his superiors in Washington in gloating terms. All that is a matter of public record. Yet, to this day, there has been no real accounting and accountability for this gruesome deed. And this is in the context of a long record of all sorts of serious human rights violations that go on to the present.

Judge Shirima reflects:

> "How does one compare those acts, which were done to satisfy an insatiable greed for profit, with what was perpetrated by the accused? They are charged under the terrorism law. But they did not cause physical harm to any person. They had idealistic intentions but were misguided into taking the law into their own hands. I think they should have been charged under lesser offenses such as damaging public and private property, and tarnishing the reputations of respected officials and citizens. In my view, making them spend the next twenty years behind bars goes against what a fair and unbiased system of justice stands for."

With such thoughts and the mitigating factors in her mind, the next day Judge Shirima imposes a sentence lighter than called for by a strict interpretation of the law. The defendants are to serve five years behind bars. To placate the prosecution and minimize the chance of being overturned on appeal, she rules that because what they did caused harm to society, the two girls will spend the time in a maximum security environment. The Judge has been guided by her conscience and the spirit, not the letter, of the law. If she has erred, she reasons, let the Court of Appeal sort it out. And she has estimated that for fear of generating further public sympathy towards the Banana Girls, the prosecutor will not appeal the lighter sentence. In this regard, she has guessed well: the prosecutor decides to put up with her decision.

Nonetheless, *Baba* and *Mama* Fatuma, and *Baba* and *Mama* Rehema cannot hold back their tears. But the media ridicule the *BLF* bandits for trying to lead the court astray at the last minute. The Mayor issues another statement:

Innocent as they look, these girls are a threat to society and do not deserve sympathy. They led 48 other young girls astray. Had we not caught them in time, more would have fallen prey to their devilish charm. They damaged property and soiled the reputation of public officials and leading philanthropists.

I ask our health experts to develop a guideline on banana consumption, especially among the children. We do not want this problem to resurface in the future.

I once more thank the American Government for the technical help in resolving this malady. I understand that long ago, it set up Banana Republics. Times have changed. I hope now it will assist us to create a Banana Free Republic.

The other members of the *BLF* are not charged in court but are made to sign an agreement whereby, for two years, they will perform assigned community service for three hours each and every day, and report to the police once per week.

Day 1499: It is the hour. Major Gama, the Warden of Udongo Prison, awaits two dangerous prisoners who will be housed at his facility. A police armada with siren blazing is at the gate. The Commissioner of Prisons and a senior Superintend of the Police have come over in person to affect the handover. As they step out of the armored holding van, the Warden gets his first look at the infamous leaders of the *Banana Liberation Front*. Having had the opportunity to receive the worst of the lot in the past, he expected two fearsome, evil-eyed persons. Instead, there are two fragile-looking things who seem to have skipped school. The two girls are shackled but bear themselves upright with dignity. It takes him an effort to suppress his smile.

"Major Gama, do not be taken in by the looks and charm of these prisoners. If you do not hold them under strict discipline, they can create havoc in this place. Is that clear?"

"Yes, sir."

"These are your orders from the Minister of Interior. They are forbidden to have contact of any form with other prisoners, an armed guard should be placed outside their door all the time, and their diet has to be completely banana free."

The Major salutes and responds:

"Yes, sir, understood sir."

He personally escorts the new inmates to their room in the isolation unit. For starters, he has decided to place them together. It makes it easier to monitor them effectively. He already faces a shortage of guards, and knows that despite the brouhaha about the special prisoners, he will not get additional funds or personnel from the HQ.

Fatuma and Rehema stand bewildered. Their room has two beds with thin sponge mattresses, but no pillows or mosquito nets. There is no other furniture, just bare walls with peeling paint. One door opens into a smelly toilet. A small window with iron bars and beyond their reach is their only connection to the world outside.

"This is our new home."

"Yes, for the next five years."

"I miss my family, so much."

"So do I, so do I."

Each one has tears running down their cheeks. They hug one another.

"But we have each other. Do not worry, we will manage."

The prison is two miles from the city. For the next few weeks, their only regular contact is the guard who brings food in the morning and evening. Major Gama comes around once a week, examines the cell, and leaves without saying a word.

One thing the girls do not want to forget is the knowledge they have acquired at the university. They have devised a scheme whereby for an hour Rehema lectures her friend on a topic from Physics or Education, and the next hour, Fatuma does so with respect to Mathematics or Development Studies. They do this on a daily basis. The guard hears strange sounds from their room and listens in. He cannot make out what they are saying and reports the matter to the warden. Major Gama as well is puzzled.

"Poor girls. I wonder if they are losing their senses."

He is surprised at the pangs of pity he feels for these dangerous convicts.

Day 1531: The Major has come for his weekly inspection. As he is about to depart, the girls address him:

"Sir, we wish to speak to you."

He looks at them sternly. It is against the rules for any inmate to speak to him unless he expressly asks him or her to do so. Yet, as both the girls stand respectfully and speak in such a gentle voice that he ignores the breach of protocol.

"Yes, what is it?"

He responds with a heavy voice.

"Sir, we have a small suggestion."

"Suggestion, you have a suggestion for me!"

"It is about food, sir."

"What about it?"

Rehema replies:

"Sir, any person's mood greatly depends on the food he eats. Everyone knows that. If the food is tasty, it will lift his spirits. If it tastes bad, he will become edgy and temperamental."

Fatuma adds:

"Sir, the prison food is bland and often tastes awful. But it can be improved with simple measures like addition of salt and lime juice."

Her friend elaborates:

"Sir, it will not cost much. We are told that the prison farm has many lime trees, and the fruit is generally not picked. The extra vitamin C will be of benefit to all in the prison."

The Major thinks to himself:

"Well, well, these upstarts have the temerity to tell me how to do my job! Do they know that I have been running this facility without any real problems for fifteen years now?"

But what they say, he concedes, makes sense. Of late, the guards have reported more disturbances in the cafeteria. It may help to try out their suggestions.

"I will think about it."

With those words, he abruptly leaves the cell. He wonders how the girls have come to know about the prison farm. The guards must be talking to them. Normally, he would investigate any breach of the rules, but decides to drop it in this case.

The senior cook says those are good ideas and requests more salt. Ten days on, the guards inform the Major that the atmosphere in the cafeteria has calmed down considerably.

Day 1559: The girls are permitted to walk about in the open compound. But it is under escort and at a time when no other prisoner is around. They find the rays of the sun, hot as they are, refreshing and nourishing. To their delight, there are three flamboyant trees in the area. They sit under one for a while. As it is the flowering season, they pluck a few unopened buds and chew the innards. The guard does not object.

Major Gama is in two minds. Though they have committed grave offenses, they remind him of his sweet daughter who is at the university. Despite what he says, she has no bad words for them, and considers them her heroines.

Day 1579: The rules read that a person in the maximum security section is allowed at most one visitor per month, and for half an hour only. The Major bends them, and allows *Mama* Rehema and *Mama* and *Baba* Fatuma to visit jointly, bring food and spend an hour with them. He also permits two more persons, former teachers or acquaintances, to visit once a month. Alternatingly, it is *Mzee* Salum with either Mr. Marufu or Mr. Felix, or Professor Chachage with Professor Kessy. The professors bring books for their self-education. Having realized that that is what the strange sounds from their room are about, the Major does not object.

After being ejected from the Batamaza school, *Mzee* Salum had spent three months in his home village. Subsequently, he resumed roasting groundnuts but now sold them in bulk to hotels and grocery stores. They paid a low price but he had no other alternative. He had heard about the trial and sentence for Fatuma and Rehema on the radio. When he approached Mr. Marufu and requested to be allowed to visit the girls in prison, his request was granted.

Day 1597: Without fail, *Mzee* Salum brings two bags of freshly roasted groundnuts, one for the girls and one for the Major. Today he is with Mr. Felix, who has the list of the first one thousand digits of π the girls had requested earlier. Having plenty of time on their hands, they plan to memorize the digits and exceed the Africa-wide record of 661 digits within six months. Mr. Felix also has a challenging numerical conundrum for his former students.

Banana Problem 4

You wish to take a pile of 3,000 bananas to a place 1,000 miles away with a camel. The camel can carry up to 1,000 bananas but will eat one banana every mile it travels (and will not go anywhere if it is not fed bananas). You can unload bananas anywhere in between. What is the most bananas you can bring over to your destination?

Smart as they are, it will take them more than a week to work out the answer. (The answer is 533 bananas. See the Banana Mathematics section.)

The visits lift their spirits. They lustily chew the nuts, sharing some with their guard. The Warden relishes the nuts. Nothing like what he has had before. He looks forward to the old man's visit as well.

Day 1607: Major Gama has an idea. Five years ago, an organization dealing with prison reform had donated a stack of books for the prison library. So far, the books have collected dust in an unused room. Maybe the girls can do something.

"Sure, Mr. Warden, we can organize the books and set up the prison library."

The next day, they are at the job. Working three hours in the morning and three in the afternoon, they clean the room, dust the books and place them in an orderly manner by subject and author on the shelves in a span of two weeks. As they list the books in a large ledger, they suggest to the Major that with a few desks and chairs, the library will be ready to use. Procured from a storage room, polished and arranged, the place has the looks of a real library. The girls are an asset to his institution.

Yet, there are practical hurdles. Who will manage the library? What of the fact that most of the prisoners can barely write their name in a legible manner?

"Sir, on Mondays, you can designate a morning hour for male prisoners to read or borrow books, and an afternoon hour for female prisoners to do the same."

"Who will supervise the library?"

"With your permission sir, we can do all that."

"Really? Just the two of you?"

"Yes sir, really."

"And sir, every Tuesday, we can lead a two-hour literacy class for the male prisoners and do likewise for female prisoners the following day."

Day 1619: So begins a new era in the prison's history. The girls have not had any contact with any other prisoner, male or female, thus far. The inmates, for their part, have only heard about two dangerous prisoners housed in the isolation unit.

The initial contact is tainted with suspicion and apprehension on both sides. But these feelings dissipate rapidly. From the second session onward, only one unarmed guard is present, and he conducts himself more like a student than a guard. The literacy classes, covering reading, writing and basic arithmetic, rise in popularity. For the first few sessions the girls take turn to read out aloud children's stories which enjoin humor, adventure and family drama. Their sonorous voices keep the audience entranced.

To ensure nothing untoward goes on, Major Gama is there in person during the entire first three sessions. He too leaves the sessions in a jovial spirit that makes him forget, at least for a while, the unending headaches of running this under-funded, overcrowded place. He also notices that the number of reported incidents of fights among the inmates or altercations between them and the guards is on the decline.

"Whatever others say, I do not think these girls have any evil bone in them. They are just ordinary girls who were temporarily led astray by some dark forces."

On the next visit, he calls *Mzee* Salum to his office to ask him why he is so devoted to these girls. The old man narrates the entire tale about their school days, and why he had to stop selling the groundnuts. Once the old man leaves, he marches to the compound. He knows the girls are there. Sure enough, they are munching the *Mzee's* nuts under a tree and chatting away. They stand up at attention as he comes near.

"You have done a wonderful job in running the library and teaching literacy. Everyone in this prison is indebted to you and thanks you."

"Sir, we thank you for giving us the opportunity to do the little we have been able to do. You had faith in us, and for that, we are truly grateful."

Major Gama pauses. Collecting his thoughts, he points to their bag of nuts, and inquires:

"Tell me, young ladies, is that what the 20 million missing nuts was about?"

It is the first time he has addressed them as he would outside these walls. They respond, instantly, softly and in unison:

"Yes sir, that is exactly what it was about."

That night, he has strange thoughts, thoughts that would never have entered his mind before. He was trained to always obey his superiors, and never question the orders given. For forty years, he has adopted that as the main credo of his life.

"How can it be? These are genuinely wonderful girls. I would take them as my daughters if I had the chance. *Mzee* Salum is a wise man who has been toiling hard throughout his life. But our leaders are treating them like they are the destroyers of our economy and way of life. Do they have the interests of our people at heart, or are they selfish politicians?"

The next day, he makes several major decisions. Thus far, as per an order from the Prison HQ, the diet of the girls has been banana free. He decides not to follow it anymore and tells the kitchen staff that they, like the rest of the prisoners, should get cooked plantains twice a week, and a sweet banana with their dinner thrice a week.

Since it was built years ago, the prison has had a large plantain and banana farm that is maintained by the inmates. It also has other crops and provides good meals for the whole prison. The prison guards buy its bananas at a low price. For a while he has thought of cutting down the banana trees, and planting sweet potatoes and cassava. But as no resources for this transition have come from the HQ, he has not implemented his plan.

Now he decides that unless he is issued a direct order, the banana farm stays. It serves his staff and the inmates. How can it be of harm? Those learned professors and the Mayor for sure are mistaken.

Day 1699: Three months earlier, Fatuma and Rehema had obtained, with the permission of the Major, two advanced books on the Theory of Relativity and Quantum Mechanics as well as writing material from Professor Kessy. In this time, they read, discussed, computed, formulated, wrote and rewrote, enduring sleepless nights in the process. Last week, with the help of *Mzee* Salum, they transmitted the product of their intellectual labor to Professor Kessy. It was a paper entitled:

Towards a Probabilistic Formulation of
the Special Theory of Relativity

Modern physics rests on two foundations, quantum mechanics and the theory of relativity. The former pertains to subatomic phenomena while the latter encompasses cosmic level events. There is, though, a major schism between the two. The former incorporates elements of randomness while the latter is a deterministic theory. There have been numerous attempts to reconcile the two foundations but none has been completely satisfactory. The banana girls have a come up with a novel approach to the issue. Professor Kessy sends the paper to *Journal of Theoretical Physics*.

Day 1721: The paper was published on the journal's website yesterday. It was an instant hit, securing a wide readership and international acclaim. Scientists everywhere are surprised and shocked to learn that the authors are young girls who have yet to finish their first degree but who are languishing in prison from a trial based on politically-motivated charges and scientifically dubious evidence. A campaign for their release ensues among the international scientific community. Yet, the mainstream media, locally and in the West, maintain a discrete silence on the matter. They do not want to be seen as supporting people who have been convicted of terrorism-related offenses. The government ignores the mountain of pleas from the same group of physicists it had earlier feted.

Day 1741: Mr. Felix and Mr. Marufu have become aware of the campaign for the girls' release but are in a quandary:

"These girls have become famous scientists; they have made Batamaza Secondary School globally known."

"And these girls are in prison, convicted of bad crimes. For that they have brought shame to their school and their teachers."

It has been a while since they last saw their former students. Today they have come to see how the two are faring. Major Gama tells them about all the good work they have been doing. The two girls cannot contain their pleasure.

On their way home, the teachers ponder on the mysteries of life.

"These were our very best students, in every respect. In spirit, they are the same, so innocent, so warm-hearted. It was as if I was talking to them at school."

"Why has fate been so cruel to them?"

Mr. Felix has concluded that the good aspects of the girls far outweigh the bad, and decides to launch and spearhead a local social media campaign to gather support from 100,000 people calling for a presidential pardon for the two. It would be on the grounds that they have already paid for their misdeeds. He is risking his job, reputation and career. But he does not want to spend the rest of his life branding himself a spineless coward.

Day 1801: While the girls have lived a secluded life, socio-political trends of destabilizing, disturbing nature have climaxed in the outside world. In the industrialized as well as the underdeveloped nations, the gap between the rich and the poor has grown astronomically over the past two decades. Giant corporations have reaped fabulous profit at the expense of workers, farmers and ordinary folk. The trends have generated unease among the masses. People are fed up with business as usual.

This social atmosphere has catalyzed two alternative political movements. One of them is propelled by socialist politicians who say that the solution lies in replacing capitalism with a society based on human solidarity, economic equality and public ownership. About a fifth of the population backs this option. However, a majority favors the authoritarian, ultra-nationalistic, strong man-based option that views outsiders and external forces as the root causes of the malaise afflicting their nation. This proto-fascistic trend has scant regard for independent media, opposition parties or fine points about the rule of law. It thrives on fear, intolerance, xenophobia, hatred and divisiveness based on race, religion, nationality and such characteristics. Important policies derive not from sound investigation and rational discourse but impromptu decisions. The pompous, yet factually-deficient pronouncements of the big banana at the helm of the state generate almost daily headlines.

While the specific features vary by nation, the trend is global. It becomes cemented as the principal ideology of the era when Ronald Grump, a political maverick with an agenda that can set the globe aflame, assumes the highest office in the United States of America. The whole world shakes in trepidation as the true, frightening colors of the man with the power to push the nuclear button come to the fore on a daily basis.

Day 1811: At the White House, Mr. Grump sips his coffee, trying to make sense of the security brief lying open before him.

"What is this project to supply advanced tanks and missiles worth two billion dollars to Vietnam? Did we not fight a war with them?"

"That was forty years ago, sir. Now they are on our side, helping us deal with our biggest foe in the region."

"And who may that be?"

"Communist China, sir."

"China? Surely you are not serious. Many of our companies, like my own, are heavily invested in China. It remains one of the few places on this blighted planet to make a good buck."

"We have to consider the bigger picture, the global geo-politics, sir."

Just at that moment, a distinguished visitor walks in, the first one to see the new boss of the nation.

"George, just in time for a fine cup of the coffee."

"Ronnie, or should I say, Mr. President, I am mighty pleased that you are not forgetting your true friends. I know that the first days in this place can be bewildering. I would not intrude, but it is an urgent matter of national security."

George Andersen is the CEO and majority shareholder of the American Banana Corporation, one of the two US firms that control over 50% of the international trade in bananas. They own large banana plantations in the Caribbean and South America and control the road and sea transport vessels that ply their products from the farm to consumers thousands of miles away.

He has been close to Ronald Grump for decades. Three months ago, when the Grump campaign was faltering, he came up with the seasoned public relations facilities of his company as well as the funds needed to mount a media blitz to rescue it.

And it had worked, stupendously. Now he seeks the payoff.

"National security, you say?"

The presidential aides nearby are totally attentive.

"Yes, Mr. President. I talk of a devious Chines conspiracy to smash to bits our majestic free enterprise system."

"How?"

"First, these commies steal our intellectual property, corrupt leaders across continents, mount unfair trade wars and engage in currency manipulation to devastate key sectors of our economy. Millions of American jobs have disappeared."

"Yes, I know that and am pledged to reverse that situation. It is on top of my list of priorities. America comes first."

"You are the leader this nation needs. I assume you know that there are some economic sectors in which we still reign supreme."

"Yes, yes."

"One of these sectors is agriculture, especially bananas. Our companies control the global market. Even the Chinese depend on us."

"Yes, yes."

"Over the past two years, the Reds have unleashed a devilish strategy to undercut our banana producing and marketing firms."

"You don't say?"

"It is unbelievable how cunning they are. They have started in an African nation that is economically insignificant but politically influential. By corrupting health officials, mayors and covertly funding a criminal gang called the *Banana Liberation Front*, they have managed to generate an anti-banana sentiment, no, anti-banana hysteria, in that place. Consumption of bananas has been declared to be at the root of many health problems. Now there are restrictions as to how many bananas a child may consume. The Mayor of the capital city is now working towards the creation of a *Banana Free Republic.*"

Ronald Grump looks at the bunch of bananas on his desk. It is his favorite snack.

"What nonsense! George, I have seen your sleek ads. I am told your boys are masters of perc... perc..., you know what I mean?"

An aide comes to the rescue:

"Perception management, sir."

"Yes, perception management. You are not trying to pull my leg, are you?"

"No, Mr. President, it sounds nonsense, but it is true."

The National Security Advisor comments:

"Mr. President, we are aware of it and it is under investigation."

The CEO goes on:

"I had alerted the previous Secretary of State several times. But I was ignored. In fact, the actions by our own embassy were crucial in bringing about that state of affairs. In the end, bananas came to be equated with terrorism. You know, our plantations in South America are affected by a deadly disease. My company was in the process of expanding its operations to Africa. The country in question was to be a major area of investment. I do not know how those sneaky Reds found out and sabotaged our plans just in the nick of time."

At this point, the senior presidential aide has a question.

"Mr. Andersen, how do you know that the Chinese were behind it?"

"It has to be. They are very clever and leave no footprint. There is no other logical explanation. Long ago, the Soviets tried to do a similar thing but we managed to prevent it."

(Mr. Andersen refers to an intense propaganda effort launched by the United Fruit Company in the 1950s to persuade the US government to intervene in Guatemala on the grounds that there was a communist conspiracy to take over that nation. A key step in that campaign was the production of the film *Why the Kremlin Hates Bananas*.)

The President has the final say.

"Yes, it makes sense. Sleep in peace, George. American jobs, man, they are a top priority on my watch. My boys will resolve the problem soon. It will be fantastic, yes, fantastic."

Day 1823: The Secretary of State teleconferences with the Director of the CIA and the head of the Centers for Disease Control. The former is tasked to uncover how the Chinese perpetrated the anti-American anti-banana plot, and the latter to inquire into the alleged banana-health-terrorism connection.

Day 1831: An epidemiologist and a nutritionist from the CDC have scrutinized the documents sent over by their embassy: the banana health study paper, the raw data from the study, interview records, media reports and assessments conducted by the embassy at that time. A critical review of the banana study is expedited for publication in next issue of *The American Journal of Public Health*.

Day 1847: Their principal finding, as summed up in the accompanying editorial of the journal, is:

The Banana Health Study is fundamentally flawed. Its conclusions lack scientific validity because (i) There was no control group; (ii) The health problems studied were identified by self-report, not accurate diagnosis; (iii) Interviews were not conducted according to standard bias reducing procedures; (iv) The study subjects were obtained via convenience sampling, not random sampling; (v) Data entry was rife with numerous errors; (vi) Statistical analysis was done using inappropriate methods; and (vii) Simple statistical association was equated with causation.

In sums, it was a classic poorly designed, oddly implemented, incorrectly analyzed and unfairly interpreted study. It had zero scientific value. The *New York Times* the next day carries the story:

Influential Banana and Health Study Debunked

Explaining the episode at length, it omits a key fact: that the study was funded and supported by the US Embassy. Neither does it note that during the trial, Fatuma and Rehema had raised objections that pointed to the flawed character of this evidence and that the voices of skeptical local scientists were muzzled. Another critical omission is that at that time American oil and gas companies were vying for lucrative contracts in the face of stiff Chinese competition. This underscored the strong backing from the US in the banana debacle. But now that the contracts have been won and signed, the so-called banana-terrorism link does not have a bearing on US interests. To the contrary, it may undermine them.

Day 1861: President Grump gives his first foreign policy speech before a throng of eager faces that had voted for him. It is classic Grump talk though its focus catches the world by surprise. His audience loves every word he has to say:

> My fellow Americans, you know that I put America first: Our vigilance has uncovered a dastardly plot to undermine a key section of our economy, bankrupt our corporations and destroy American jobs. It is too fantastic but we have proof the Chinese are behind it. They funded a terror group in Africa called the *Banana Liberation Front* and used health experts to bring bananas into disrepute. By working on both sides, they achieved their objective: to tarnish the image of a staple of our economy, a product in which our companies lead the global market and which contributes tens of thousands of jobs for our citizens. Can you believe it?

> This time the Reds have crossed the red line, yes; they have crossed the red line. It is an act of war. It is unforgivable. They must pay the price. First, I am imposing a tariff of 10% on all Chinese agricultural items imported into the US. Second, I want the Chinese Government to come clean and issue a formal apology. Else, I will take harsher measures, yes, harsher measures.

And here, to the dismay of his staff, he veers totally off the script:

> It is unbelievable. My democratic opponent and the previous occupant of this office, yes both of them, blessed the Chinese plot. It is shocking, most shocking. Are they loyal Americans? I wonder. I have asked the FBI to look into it. They talk of me, a true blooded American, as if I am a part of some Russian conspiracy. Look at what they were up to; yes, look at it.

The presidential address raises alarm and shock in Beijing. The mood is both grave as well as comical.

"Bananas? What did we ever have to do with bananas?"

China had hosted an international conference on banana diseases two years ago. The American Banana Corporation had been one of its sponsors and many American, British and European scientists had participated in it. It was the only major banana-related event that had occurred in China in the last two decades.

"How can that be connected to any form of terrorism?"

"Have bananas become the new Weapons of Mass Destruction? You know, the ones they swore were there in Iraq but were never found. Is this man going bananas? Most likely, it is an excuse to go to war."

As a precautionary measure, the armed forces of China are placed on the highest state of alert. The nuclear missiles are set on instant launch status as well.

Day 1867: Back in the African nation, the US ambassador meets top government officials and conveys a stern message.

"Our national security is at stake. The banana craziness has to stop, and right away. Else, in two weeks, we will cease all our projects and financial assistance to you."

The effect is immediate. First the Ministry of Health issues a statement declaring that the findings of the banana study were highly misleading. A commission of inquiry is set to inquire how such a study could have been done and the entire nation led astray. The Mayor who dreams of a *Banana Free Republic* realizes that his days are numbered, and hands in his resignation to avoid further embarrassment.

Day 1871: The banana is officially declared as a health enhancing food. The new mayor lifts the restrictions placed on fruit and vegetable vendors the day after he assumes office. Now they can go back to doing what they were doing before. *Baba* Fatuma begins weeding his neglected banana farm and selling his prized fruit once more.

There is another side to this story. National and municipal elections are a year away. Unemployment, especially among the youth, remains an intractable problem. The blanket ban on street vendors has just exacerbated it. The ruling party is aware that it is in danger of losing a sizeable portion of the urban and peri-urban vote to the opposition parties. Lifting the ban may prevent a potential electoral calamity. At least for the next twelve months, the vendors can breathe a sigh of relief.

Day 1877: Rehema and Fatuma receive a presidential pardon. Major Gama personally drives them home in a prison jeep. He is happy for them but feels a tinge of sadness too. He has become so used to their presence. The prisoners and the staff will miss them too. Will he see his two daughters again?

Mama Fatuma exclaims in joy:

"*Mungu Wangu*, my child has come home."

Mother and daughter hug each other as if for eternity, tears inundating their faces. *Baba* Fatuma is away selling his wares, and Ali is at school. He now goes to Batamaza school, she learns. *Mama* tells her about the financial assistance they have been getting from Alice.

When Ali returns, he is overcome with joy. Dancing and jumping about her, he chants:

"*Dada, dada, dada, dada* ...."

When *Baba* returns, he just stands like a statue for a while, staring at her. Then, upon placing his hands on her shoulders, he abruptly goes outside. He does not want his family to see the tears forming in his eyes.

At dinner time, Ali is all talk. He wants to know where she has been, what she was doing and if she missed him or not. He keeps on as they retire for the night on their mattresses, telling her about his school, the soccer matches he has played for his grade team and the fight he had with a boy in the neighborhood who wanted to take away his soccer ball. He was bruised but managed to hold on to his ball. His symphony of words goes on until their eyes cannot take it anymore and they are transported into the dream world.

A similar scene transpires between Rehema and her *Mama*.

"You have become so thin, my baby."

"I will be fine, *Mama*, now that I will have your delicious food every day. I am craving for your *kuku pilau*."

"You will have it right this evening."

"Where is *Baba*?"

"Your *Baba* is inside."

She finds him lying on his bed. She hugs him and he holds her tightly, uttering:

"My child, my child, my child."

His face is wet, but he does not say anything else.

When they come out, *Mama* Rehema tells her:

"Eight months ago, your *Baba* was involved in an altercation with a group of coconut sellers. One of them threw a coconut at him. It hit him on his head. He was knocked unconscious and was taken to hospital. Since then he has not been able to do anything. Most days, he is in bed, and only says something when he is hungry. It is the first time he said anything else."

Now Rehema understands why her *Baba* did not visit her when she was in prison. She has suddenly lost her craving for *kuku pilau*.

Day 1879: *Baba* is home early to weed his *shamba*. Ali and Fatuma are helping out; she makes piles of the cut weeds while he carries them to a corner. The rainy season is approaching. During a heavy downpour, the farm gets water logged, which is not good for the banana plants. *Baba* is also digging a drainage channel from the center to a low lying corner. His children assist by dispersing the sand and gravel he has dug across the backyard.

Baba tells Fatuma that he does not sell bananas door-to-door as he used to. It is too tiring for him now. He has been lucky to be allocated a stall at a local market where he sells bananas, tomatoes, onions and carrots. These other vegetables he buys in bulk from the neighbor's farm.

He pays a monthly rental of 10,000 shillings to the market management. The business has been good and steady. He has informed his old customers about his location, so they too come now and then to get his prized bananas and plantains.

Nevertheless, he cannot stop thinking about the banana beer he used to brew. He asks Fatuma, whose opinion he has come to respect:

> "With the new mayor, do you think the city will lift the restriction on homemade alcohol the way it charged its stand on street sellers?"

> "*Baba*, I am sorry to say I don't think so. The big breweries do not like that kind of competition. They want the entire market for themselves. Even for street vendors, you never know what will happen after the election. You know these politicians, one day they do this and the next, quite the opposite."

> "I am glad I have a market stall now."

Day 1913: Fatuma, Rehema and Alice are readmitted at the university. They pass the final year examination with flying colors and join the academic staff of that august institution. The changed political environment combined with their outstanding scholarship comes to outweigh the misgivings the university administration has about their past deeds.

Day 1949: On the first day at work, they are profoundly saddened to learn that Professor Chachage has passed on. His example and what he taught them will remain indelibly ingrained in their psyche. Like him, they will strive to be dedicated, inspiring and competent teachers who will do research that will take them to the frontiers of their disciplines and also serve the nation. Their first major applied research project, conducted in conjunction with the Ministry of Industry, the Ministry of Agriculture and two colleagues from the School of Engineering, is about the feasibility of producing paper from the banana plant.

Day 1973: Mr. George Andersen, the CEO of the American Banana Corporation, is in town on a much ballyhooed visit. For the past two days, he has monopolized the lead media stories. Yesterday he had made well publicized visits to an orphanage and a school for disabled children and donated supplies worth 5,000 US dollars. The philanthropic gesture draws accolades from many quarters, including faith groups of all denominations.

Today he sits alongside a decorated negotiation table with the US ambassador at his side and the Minister of Agriculture and the Minister of Foreign Affairs across from him. Each side has six aides in attendance. A major investment agreement with an initial outlay of US$50 million is about to be signed. Under this deal, the American Banana Corporation will establish two banana plantations, each eventually spanning five thousand hectares, one in the northern coastal area and the other in the southern coastal area. The bananas produced will primarily cater to the export market with the aim of turning the nation into Africa's largest exporter of the fruit within five years. Thousands of jobs will be created as a result. The farmers currently in these areas will be relocated to other productive lands and will be compensated adequately. It is all smiles around the table as ink is put to paper. A gala dinner for local and visiting dignitaries hosted by the US embassy this evening will climax the trip.

That is what is publicized. Not mentioned are the facts that the company will have a 99-year irrevocable lease on the land and will pay no tax or export duty for five years. People also know that promises to relocate and compensate people displaced by foreign investors in the past have not lived up to the initial hype and the compensation payments take years to materialize. But print and broadcast media remain silent on such shortcomings. The US embassy regularly holds parties for local journalists; none of them wants to find himself or herself disinvited and miss out the rounds of beer and wine. Professor Chachage, had he been alive, would have raised, in public and with a loud voice, critical concerns like worker benefits, health and welfare, the economic impact on small scale banana producers, the spread of banana disease and environmental consequences of the plantation mode of production. He would have highlighted the historical record of this company in Central America. But his voice is no more. The other intellectuals of his stature are preoccupied with churning out dubious quality papers hardly anyone, other than possibly the members of their promotion committee, will read.

At a news conference held prior to his departure, an American reporter asks Mr. Andersen:

> "Are you still worried about the Chinese plot to undermine your company?"

He responds with a seasoned smile:

> "That is a matter for our political leaders. I am a businessman, not a politician. Presently, the popularity of our quality bananas is rising in China. I have no qualms about expanding this mutually beneficial relationship."

While there is unease at the grassroots level, prominent businessmen in the African nation look forward to lucrative subcontracts with the banana plantations. Alice's brother wants to clinch the exclusive rights to maintain, repair and supply spare parts for what is envisaged to be a sizable plantation vehicular fleet. Upon hearing about that plan, Alice tells him about the deeds of the company in Latin America. But Jonathan cuts her off:

> "Sis, I am not into history. This is business. You don't get far if you worry about such things."

"But it is important for our country."

"Look, sis, your wild ideas almost landed you in prison. Only *Baba*'s influence saved you. It is high time you joined the family business. You will be a director of something and earn five times what you get now. It will be a good life."

When he sees that she is unhappy, he places his hands on her shoulders and tries to appease her:

"Sis, you look tired. Let me take you for dinner at the new roof garden restaurant. The view is spectacular and they serve top class Italian food."

She declines, saying she has to prepare her lectures for the next day and withdraws to her room.

Day 1997: Fatuma and Rehema have fulfilled their promise to Major Gama. For three days last week, they went to the Udongo Prison to train two female inmates to run the prison library. In addition, they have recruited eight former members of the *BLF*, including Alice, to conduct weekly literacy classes at the prison. They will go in pairs, taking turns. Major Gama will provide transport to and from the prison.

Day 1999: It is Pi Day once again, an event marked in schools in all continents. It has become an annual feature at Batamaza Secondary School as well. Today, though, it is a special day in ways more than one. Mr. Marufu is set to retire at the end of the month. So it is the last time he will oversee the event. Mr. Felix, who is as popular and eminently qualified, will be the new headmaster. Initially, the Ministry of Education was not in favor of promoting him to that position. His campaign for the release of the imprisoned girls had displeased the ministry officials. But the altered socio-political climate and the rehabilitation of the Banana Girls had changed everything. To top it all, Fatuma and Rehema are the guests of honor today.

At break time, the girls are delighted to note that the food vendors are at the school gate once again. Mr. Marufu, to his credit, had successfully managed to block the setting up of a junk food snack shop within the school grounds. There had been unrelenting pressure from the District Education Officer. He had said he would find a room for the shop, but never did. There had been a drought of a sort at the school but now there was plenty.

Mzee Salum, however, is not there. He has developed knee pain and is unable to walk long distances. Instead, his son now comes to sell the *karanga* he roasts and packages at home. The nuts are as delicious as ever. Fatuma and Rehema purchase two packages and tell the young man that they will visit his father next week.

Another thing that brings smiles to their faces is that Mrs. Kamala has initiated a *Mkakaya* planting project at the school. Besides tree, eleven other *Mkakaya*s have been placed around the school soccer playground. The new ones are but tiny stalks at present. Four to five Form I biology students tend to each growing plant. They dug the holes, mixed the soil with fertilizer and now, under the supervision of *Mzee* Simon, water their plants. As they will be at the school for the next four years, they may see their charge perhaps reach their heights. The tall, flowering trees will take many more years to emerge, yet it will be an invaluable legacy for the generations to come.

The contest for memorization of the digits of π takes place in the afternoon. Two Form VI students emerge as the winners by accurately reciting the first 271 digits. It is a new school record. Then comes the climax. Rehema steps out of the hall. Fatuma goes on the stage and recites, without error, the first 1009 digits of π. Subsequently Rehema repeats the same feat. Both have set a new African record. The recitations occur in the presence of an independent panel of five judges and are recorded. Hence they will be submitted for official recognition.

At the end of their recitations, the Banana Girls hand out photocopied sheets of paper containing a bananaized version of the digits of Pi. It generates ripples of laughter from the students.

Day 2003: Fatuma and Rehema are at Professor Chachage's house, at a memorial event in his honor. Former students and colleagues narrate inspiring incidents from unique life and recall his accomplishments. Officials of the university administration, with whom he was perpetually at odds, are conspicuous by their absence. Ill at ease with his iconoclastic ideas and social activism, they had regularly tried to block his promotion to a higher academic rank. But his scholarly output had been so prolific and of singular quality that their efforts always came to naught.

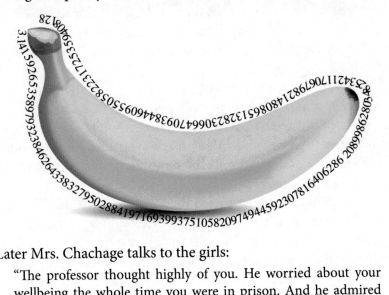

Later Mrs. Chachage talks to the girls:

"The professor thought highly of you. He worried about your wellbeing the whole time you were in prison. And he admired the way you conducted yourselves with dignity under the most difficult of circumstances."

"It was an honor for us that he was our mentor and guide. Had we not met him, our lives would have been much poorer."

"He has left a vast library of books on many different subjects. I am sorting and packing them so as to donate them to the libraries of teacher training colleges and other educational institutions. But I have set aside these five books for you. I am sure the professor would have wanted me to do this."

She gives them a plastic bag containing the books. The girls smile at the same time as they hold back their tears. When they reach their campus office, they see that one of books is Dana Frank's *Bananeras: Women Transforming the Banana Unions of Latin America*. It portrays the exemplary role played by women in the decades-long struggle for basic rights and social justice for the workers in the banana plantations of South and Central America. It is the book each one of them wants to read first. So they toss a coin to determine who will be the lucky one.

Day 2003: It being a public holiday, Fatuma's two buddies are visiting her at home. Ali is playing soccer with neighborhood kids. *Baba* is at a friend's place two doors away playing *bao* and sipping strong *kahawa*. *Mama* is fully occupied cooking a big meal for the family and friends. Alice has brought two kilos of lamb meat, which Fatuma's family has never had before. So it will be feast of *ndizi na nyama* cooked in coconut milk. Fatuma volunteers to help. *Mama* says she can manage and tells her to be with her friends.

Alice, Fatuma and Rehema sit in the back porch of Fatuma's home that overlooks the *shamba*. A gentle breeze reflects their mood. They talk of the past, present and future.

"Do you have any regrets?"

"None, none at all."

"We made some mistakes and broke the law. But we acted with good intent."

"In future, we should avoid such mistakes."

"But we should not forget our concern for our fellow human beings and the welfare of the nation."

They are aware that one big danger that faces the nation is that it is likely on the road to becoming Africa's first Banana Republic. They well know the atrocious historical record of the American Banana Corporation in Latin America, and have no reason to believe that it will act differently in Africa. Profits before all else: that is the enduring prime capitalist ethic. The consequences for the small farmers, plantation workers, the environment and the health of the national banana sector will be, they feel, highly deleterious.

The three girls (rather, women one should say) are prepared to play their role in preventing the materialization of that state of affairs. Using legal and peaceful means, they hope to work with other citizens and social rights organizations to raise public awareness and protect the rights and welfare of farmers and workers. For one thing, they have the inspiring example of the *Bananeras* of the Latin America. They plan to reach out to their compatriots across the oceans, initially through the Internet and later perhaps in person to learn directly from their experience and wisdom. If corporations can globalize, why cannot the workers and their advocates? When spirits are in unison, language is no barrier.

They say organizations can be banned but ideals and ideas live on. Correspondingly, the spirit of the *Banana Liberation Front* is alive and vibrant.

The digits of the enigmatic transcendental number π have no end. Yet, π is encapsulated within each circle. It has infinite and finite facets. Alice, Fatuma and Rehema likewise are at the threshold of a lifelong journey, an unpredictable, challenge-filled, meandering journey. They hope that if they adhere to a steadfast, humane vision, it will be a fulfilling journey. With the wisdom of Albert Einstein as their guide, they are ready to take the plunge:

A hundred times every day I remind myself
that my inner and outer lives depend on the
labors of other men, a live or dead, and that
I must exert myself in order to give in the same
measure as I have received and am still receiving.

Albert Einstein

Not that it matters for now. The aroma of *Mama's matoke* blows in the wind. Ali is back, poised to bombard them with questions and brag about how he scored the winning goal today. Rehema has brought two multi-subject school notebooks for Ali. He exclaims:

"*Ahsante, dada*, they are just what I needed."

Baba has returned with a giant-sized watermelon. As he slices it, *Mama* beckons the trio. A sumptuous feast awaits.

As they relish the culinary delight, Ali is unusually silent. He seems to be muttering something. All of a sudden, he stands up:

"*Baba, Mama, dada* Alice, *dada* Rehema and *dada* Fatuma, I have something to say."

"Say it, my son."

Ali recites the first twenty four digits of π,

$$3.14159265358979323846264$$

pauses for a couple of seconds, and recites them backwards

$$46264832397985356295141.3$$

It is a remarkable accomplishment, indicative of a creative spirit. The three girls clap their hands and his parents do the same, though they do not know what is going on.

"I can do it for thirty digits."

"Then why did you stop at twenty four?"

"Because it is *dada* Fatuma's twenty fourth birthday tomorrow. This is my present for her."

He gets a pat on his cheek.

"It is so sweet of you, Ali."

"By the coming π-day, I want to be able to do that for fifty digits. I hope Mr. Felix will allow me to recite them at the event."

Ali represents Africa's emergent youth. Fed up with injustice and poverty, they are on the march. Not content with piecemeal steps, their goal is to turn the current ugly reality upside down.

SUPPLEMENTARY MATERIAL

BANANA BASICS

Bananas occur in over a thousand varieties. For the consumer, though, they are of two basic types: those that can be eaten directly (eating bananas) and those that need to be cooked (cooking bananas). The term 'banana' at times refers to just the former type, and at times, includes both types. Eating bananas are cooked as well. Cooking bananas include plantains and other varieties.

This section provides some basic facts about bananas. Unless otherwise stated, here the term 'banana' covers both types of bananas.

1. Archaeological evidence indicates that banana cultivation began in Asia some 10,000 years ago. Today, it is the fourth most cultivated crop and the most consumed fruit on the planet. Most of the production occurs in the tropical and subtropical nations of Asia, Africa, South America, the Caribbean and the Pacific region.

2. India produces more bananas than any other nation, accounting for a fifth of the global total. Uganda has the highest per capita consumption of bananas. In such nations, bananas are grown mostly in small farms and hardly any are exported. In nations like Honduras, bananas are grown in plantations, over 90 percent are exported and the trade is dominated by a few US corporations. Consumers in North America and Europe basically eat imported bananas.

3. Bananas have green, yellow, red or other-coloured skins. Their high nutritional value is due to good levels of fibre and key vitamins and minerals. Non-sweet cooking bananas are recommended by health experts for prevention of chronic lifestyle diseases, and, due to their low glycemic index, are said to be useful for diabetics as well.

4. The banana skin is edible. Parts of the banana plant are used for making cloth, paper, dyes and other products.

5. Bananas are added to dessert, bread, cake, juice, ice cream etc., and roasted, fried, or otherwise cooked in a diversity of culturally specific styles. In some areas, they are brewed into mild or potent alcoholic drinks.

6. In places where it has taken root, the banana has become a part of the local culture and is integrated into local beliefs, songs, poetry, folklore, movies and idiom. The first music album to sell over a million copies worldwide was Harry Belafonte's *Calypso*. The album includes his magnificent rendition of *The Banana Boat Song*.

7. Growing bananas in large plantations has raised productivity and lowered the cost for the Western consumer. But this has occurred in conjunction with decades of massive human rights abuse and brutality perpetrated by US corporations, agencies of the US government and authoritarian regimes. The plantation workers are exposed to harmful chemicals without protection for extended hours, low wages and hardly any benefits. Banana union leaders and activists have been targeted by right wing death squads for a long time. Child labour is a serious malady afflicting banana cultivation across the world.

8. The production of a standard type of banana under uniform, monoculture, plantation conditions makes it susceptible, in the long run, to deadly disease that can spread widely and wipe out the entire variety. This event first occurred in the 1930s and is now at the industry's door step once again.

9. A sustainable and humane future for bananas lies in small scale production with the preservation of existent varieties, minimal use of chemicals and pesticides, and timely support to the farmers. And this has to occur with organization of efficient regional distribution networks in which the growers, transport workers and small vendors get adequate returns for their labor. But this cannot occur just for a single crop. Further, it is a highly improbable scenario under the neo-liberal economic order that prevails in all the national and international economies today.

10. Modern capitalism thrives on an irrational and unethical form of consumerism whereby appearance is valued over content. Thus the British people discard 1.4 million "edible bananas every day, apparently because they have small black, brown or green marks on the skin." Hanson (2017). Yet, poverty and hunger are on the rise in the UK. In any African nation, such a practice would be considered to be bordering on madness.

11. Another unpleasant practice associated with the banana is its use in Europe and America as a racist symbol against prominent African and black-skinned sports, cultural and political personalities. Despite the imposition of sanctions, these sorts of ugly incidents continue to be reported.

For further information on the biology, agronomy, culture, food preparation aspects, history and the socio-economic reality of the banana, see the books in the reading list, and the following web based sources. In my judgment, these sources are mostly free from corporate bias.

A. www.wikipedia.org

B. www.promusa.org

C. www.bananalink.org.uk

D. www.britannica.com/plant/banana-plant

E. www.globalissues.org
F. http://www.naturalnews.com/032794_Dole_bananas.html
G. http://www.nytimes.com/2002/07/13/world/in-ecuador-s-banana-fields-child-labor-is-key-to-profits.html
H. http://earthfirstjournal.org/newswire/2015/03/20/costa-rica-banana-workers-ongoing-strike-hopes-to-bring-attention-to-worker-abuse/
I. http://www.ghrc-usa.org/Publications/ArbenzBananaFactSheet.pdf
J. http://www.greens.org/s-r/17/17-10.html
K. http://members.tripod.com/foro_emaus/p1ing.htm
L. https://www.thenation.com/article/banana-kings/
M. http://www.veganpeace.com/sweatshops/sweatshops_and_child_labor.htm
N. http://jrscience.wcp.muohio.edu/fieldcourses04/PapersCostaRicaArticles/GoingBananas.thebananaind.html
O. http://www.coha.org/peeling-back-the-truth-on-the-guatemalan-banana-industry/

Another recommended strategy to obtain well-rounded, current, accessible and comprehensive information about bananas is to conduct a search under the term 'banana' at the website www.theguardian.com.

BANANA CULTURE

Wherever they are cultivated or consumed in large quantities, bananas have become a part of the local culture and tradition. They feature in songs, folklore, humor, beliefs, movies and culinary collections. Even scientists and mathematicians use them to explicate their ideas.

This section gives two songs and two poems connected to the banana that are internationally acclaimed together with a plantain recipe from East Africa. Since there are many Internet sites that have these items, no particular source is given.

Banana Sellers' Song

This children's song is popular in nursery and primary schools of East Africa. It is sung alternately in Swahili and English and is repeated two to three times.

Swahili	English
Ndizi machungwa	Bananas oranges
Ndizi machungwa	Bananas oranges
Tunayauza	We are selling them
Tunayauza	We are selling them
Nani yutaka	Who wants some?
Nani yutaka	Who wants some?

The Banana Boat Song

The Banana Boat Song originated from the chants of the work gangs loading bananas onto ships anchored in the Jamaican harbor. Toiling by night, they yearn for daylight so as to get their pay and head home. The words have been rendered into song by several artists. The best known is the one by the eminent calypso singer and civil rights activist, Harry Belafonte, released in 1956.

Day O

Day-o, day-ay-ay-o
Daylight come and he wan' go home
Day, he say day, he say day, he say day, he say day, he say
day-ay-ay-o
Daylight come and he wan' go home

Work all night on a drink a'rum
(Daylight come and he wan' go home)
Stack banana till thee morning come
(Daylight come and he wan' go home)

Come, Mr. Tally Mon, tally me banana
(Daylight come and he wan' go home)

Come, Mr. Tally Mon, tally me banana
(Daylight come and he wan' go home)

It's six foot, seven foot, eight foot, BUNCH!
(Daylight come and he wan' go home)
Six foot, seven foot, eight foot, BUNCH!
(Daylight come and he wan' go home)

Day, he say day-ay-ay-o
(Daylight come and he wan' go home)
Day, he say day, he say day, he say day,
He say day, he say day
(Daylight come and he wan' go home)

A beautiful bunch a'ripe banana
(Daylight come and he wan' go home)
Hide thee deadly black tarantula
(Daylight come and he wan' go home)

It's six foot, seven foot, eight foot, BUNCH!
(Daylight come and he wan' go home)
Six foot, seven foot, eight foot, BUNCH!
(Daylight come and he wan' go home)

Day, he say day-ay-ay-o
(Daylight come and he wan' go home)
Day, he say day, he say day, he say day,
He say day, he say day
(Daylight come and he wan' go home)

Come, Mr. Tally Mon, tally me banana
(Daylight come and he wan' go home)
Come, Mr. Tally Mon, tally me banana
(Daylight come and he wan' go home)

Day-o, day-ay-ay-o
(Daylight come and he wan' go home)
Day, he say day, he say day, he say day, he say day, he say
day-ay-ay-o
(Daylight come and he wan' go home)

The Song of the Banana Man

The Song of the Banana Man, a poem-cum-song composed by Evan Jones, is set in the hilly terrain of Jamaica of the 1940s. A small scale banana farmer proudly reflects on his life and work, fraught with hardship as they are. Though rendered in the lingo of Jamaican Creole, its accessibility and appeal are universal. It is widely available on the Internet in the form of poetry recital, lyrics and analysis.

The Song of the Banana Man

Touris, white man, wipin his face,
Met me in Golden Grove market place.
He looked at m'ol' clothes brown wid stain ,
An soaked right through wid de Portlan rain,
He cas his eye, turn up his nose,
He says, 'You're a beggar man, I suppose?'
He says, 'Boy, get some occupation,
Be of some value to your nation.'
I said, 'By God and dis big right han
You mus recognize a banana man.
'Up in de hills, where de streams are cool,
An mullet an janga swim in de pool,
I have ten acres of mountain side,
An a dainty-foot donkey dat I ride,
Four Gros Michel, an four Lacatan,
Some coconut trees, and some hills of yam,
An I pasture on dat very same lan
Five she-goats an a big black ram,
Dat, by God an dis big right han
Is de property of a banana man.

'I leave m'yard early-mornin time
An set m'foot to de mountain climb,
I ben m'back to de hot-sun toil,
An m'cutlass rings on de stony soil,
Ploughin an weedin, diggin an plantin
Till Massa Sun drop back o John Crow mountain,

Den home again in cool evenin time,
Perhaps whistling dis likkle rhyme,
(Sung)Praise God an m'big right han
I will live an die a banana man.

Banana day is my special day,
I cut my stems an I'm on m'way,
Load up de donkey, leave de lan
Head down de hill to banana stan,
When de truck comes roun I take a ride
All de way down to de harbour side—
Dat is de night, when you, touris man,
Would change your place wid a banana man.
Yes, by God, an m'big right han
I will live an die a banana man.

'De bay is calm, an de moon is bright
De hills look black for de sky is light,
Down at de dock is an English ship,
Restin after her ocean trip,
While on de pier is a monstrous hustle,
Tallymen, carriers, all in a bustle,
Wid stems on deir heads in a long black snake
Some singin de sons dat banana men make,
Like, (Sung) Praise God an m'big right han
I will live an die a banana man.

'Den de payment comes, an we have some fun,
Me, Zekiel, Breda and Duppy Son.
Down at de bar near United Wharf
We knock back a white rum, bus a laugh,
Fill de empty bag for further toil
Wid saltfish, breadfruit, coconut oil.
Den head back home to m'yard to sleep,
A proper sleep dat is long an deep.
Yes, by God, an m'big right han
I will live an die a banana man.

'So when you see dese ol clothes brown wid stain,
An soaked right through wid de Portlan rain,
Don't cas your eye nor turn your nose,
Don't judge a man by his patchy clothes,
I'm a strong man, a proud man, an I'm free,
Free as dese mountains, free as dis sea,
I know myself, an I know my ways,
An will sing wid pride to de end o my days
(Sung)Praise God an m'big right han
I will live an die a banana man.'

The United Fruit Company

The United Fruit Company, a searing poem by the Chilean Nobel laurate Pablo Neruda, focuses on the brutal behavior of the United States in supporting dictators and promoting the interests of rapacious US corporations like the Boston-based United Fruit Company. It mentions the dictators and alludes to the tragic history of South America and Central America, and notes the continued exploitation of their peoples. The version below is a translation from the Spanish original.

The United Fruit Company

When the trumpet sounded, it was
all prepared on the earth,
the Jehovah parceled out the earth
to Coca Cola, Inc., Anaconda,
Ford Motors, and other entities:
The Fruit Company, Inc.
reserved for itself the most succulent,
the central coast of my own land,
the delicate waist of America.
It rechristened its territories
as the 'Banana Republics'
and over the sleeping dead,
over the restless heroes
who brought about the greatness, the liberty and the flags,
it established the comic opera:
abolished the independencies,

presented crowns of Caesar,
unsheathed envy, attracted
the dictatorship of the flies,
Trujillo flies, Tacho flies,
Carias flies, Martines flies,
Ubico flies, damp flies
of modest blood and marmalade,
drunken flies who zoom
over the ordinary graves,
circus flies, wise flies
well trained in tyranny.

Among the blood-thirsty flies
the Fruit Company lands its ships,
taking off the coffee and the fruit;
the treasure of our submerged
territories flow as though
on plates into the ships.

Meanwhile Indians are falling
into the sugared chasms
of the harbors, wrapped
for burials in the mist of the dawn:
a body rolls, a thing
that has no name, a fallen cipher,
a cluster of the dead fruit
thrown down on the dump.

A Banana Recipe

A commonly prepared bananas meal in East Africa is variously called *Matoke, Mtori,* or *Ndizi na Nyama.* While often cooked with meat, it is also made with fish, nuts or beans. Some cooks add coconut milk, others do not. Below is a basic non-meat recipe.

Vegetarian *Matoke*

1. Boil a cup and a half of pre-soaked small red beans OR groundnuts until soft. Set aside.

2. Peel and cut seven large cooking bananas and place them in water.

3. Chop two large onions and two large tomatoes. Fry them in oil until soft. Add garlic paste, turmeric, salt and other spices according to taste. Two minutes on, add the beans or groundnuts, and cook for five to ten minutes. Add water if the mixture becomes too dry.

4. Finally add the cut bananas. Cook until well done. You may add lime juice to the dish. Serve hot.

BANANA MATHEMATICS

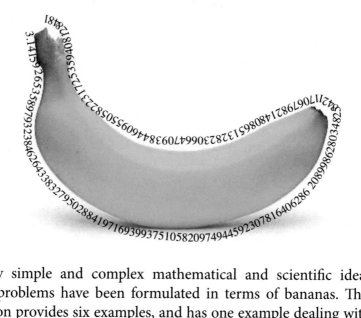

Many simple and complex mathematical and scientific ideas and problems have been formulated in terms of bananas. This section provides six examples, and has one example dealing with groundnuts. Four of these appear in the main text. They are given with solutions. The remaining ones are open ended and more practical. The examples are followed by information about the mathematical constant π.

Banana Problem 1

Fatima is walking home with a lion, a monkey and a bunch of bananas. Halfway, she has to cross a river. In addition to herself, the small boat can take only one of the three. The monkey cannot be left with the bananas, and the lion cannot be left with the monkey. How can she make the crossing?

Solution: First she takes the monkey across and returns alone. Then she takes the lion across and returns with the monkey. Then she takes the bananas across and returns alone. Finally she takes the monkey across.

Banana Problem 2

Hungry *Baba Nyani* enters the kitchen at night and eats 1/6 of a banana bunch. At dawn, *Mama Nyani* feasts on 1/5 of what remains. *Kaka Nyani* gobbles up 1/4 of what he finds upon return from night work, and *Dada Nyani* is satisfied with 1/3 of what is there. *Mtoto Nyani* is content with half of what *Dada* has left for him. After he has had his share, 7 bananas remain. How many bananas were there at the outset?

Solution: If X was the number of bananas at the outset, then the number in the bunch at each stage was as follows:

Bananas	Eaten By	Amount
X	Baba	X/6
5X/6	Mama	X/6
4X/6	Kaka	X/6
3X/6	Dada	X/6
2X/6	Mtoto	X/6
X/6	Remaining	7

Hence, X/6 = 7 and X = 42

We can declare that this is a fair minded family as everyone ate the same number of bananas.

Banana Problem 3

Asha buys 3 bananas and 4 mangoes for 2,900 shillings; Alice buys 4 bananas and 3 mangoes for 2,700 shillings. Janet has to buy 5 bananas and 5 mangoes. How much money does she need?

Solution: Let b and m be the prices of a banana and a mango, respectively. Then

$$3b + 4m = 2900$$

$$4b + 3m = 2700$$

Solving these equations, we get b = 300 and m = 500. Then we find that

$$5b + 5m = 4000$$

Hence Janet will need 4,000 shillings for her purchase.

Banana Problem 4

You have a pile of 3,000 bananas. You wish to transport them to a place 1,000km away on the back of a camel. The camel can carry a maximum of 1,000 bananas, and will eat one banana every kilometer it travels (and does not move without bananas). You can load and unload bananas at any point. What is the maximum number of bananas you can deposit at your destination?

Solution: Let A and B be two stations between the origin and the destination. A lies 200 km from the origin and B is 333 km from A. (i) Take 1000 bananas to A, deposit 600, and return with 200. (ii) Take 1000 bananas to A, deposit 600, and return with 200. (iii) Take 1000 bananas to A and deposit 800. You have 2,000 bananas at A. (iv) Take 1000 bananas to B, deposit 334 and return to A with 333. (v) Take 1000 bananas to B, and deposit 667. (vi) Of the 1,001 bananas at B, eat 1 and transport 1,000 to the destination, which is 467 km away. Hence you arrive at the destination with 533 bananas.

A proof that this is the best solution is given at many websites. See http://puzzle.dse.nl/math/bananas_us.html.

Problem 5

Asha buys 3 bananas, 4 mangoes and 5 oranges for 4,100 shillings; Alice buys 5 bananas, 4 mangoes and 3 oranges for 3,900 shillings; Ali buys 5 bananas, 4 mangoes and 4 oranges for 4,200 shillings. Janet has to buy 7 bananas, 6 mangoes and 5 oranges. How much money does she need?

Solution Hint: Formulate three linear equations in three unknowns and solve to find the price of each fruit. These prices will tell you that Janet needs 5,900 shillings for her fruit basket.

Banana Problem 6

Estimate the number of groundnuts in the picture below. Then have 10 different people make 10 independent estimates. What do you conclude from these 11 estimates?

Repeat the exercise with a pile of similar size whose picture you have taken. Count the groundnuts in this pile. Use this information to comment on the reliability of the previous estimates.

Suppose you need a good estimate of the number of groundnuts in a 100 kg bag. How will you get it without counting the entire lot?

Banana Problem 7

District X has 30 banana-growing villages. You need a reasonable estimate of the annual tonnage of bananas produced in the district. Each of your 10 research assistants can cover only one village and spend at most 5 days at the site. Work out a detailed plan to accomplish your objective.

On Pi

The mathematical constant Pi, denoted π, is the ratio of the circumference of a circle to its diameter. It has numerous applications in all branches of science, engineering, research and other areas of mathematics. Expanded in a decimal form, the digits of π go on forever. In a testimony to human ingenuity, over 12 trillion digits had been calculated and stored in electronic form by the year 2012. If these digits were laid out in a straight line with each digit 2 mm wide, the line would stretch from the earth to the moon and back 12 times.

Memorization of the digits of π is a marathon like mental challenge for students and enthusiasts the world over. At least until March 2017, the world record in this endeavor was held by Suresh K Sharma of India. In October 2015, he recited from memory and without error 70,030 digits of π. It took him 17 hours and 14 minutes to accomplish this feat. The previous record holder was Rajveer Meena, also from India, who seven months earlier had recited 70,000 digits.

Africa lags far behind and has yet to conquer the 1,000 digit barrier. The main reason for this sorry state of affairs is neglect on the part of local mathematical organizations and educators. Reciting, say, 200 digits of π from memory can be done by most people (Foer 2012). What are required are will, encouragement, determination, regular practice and the use of appropriate techniques. One helpful technique is to group the digits into sets of two to five digits, forming some sort of pattern where possible and working on memorizing three to five sets at a time. Many Internet sites and books explain these memory enhancing techniques. One site is

www.geom.uiuc.edu/~huberty/math5337/groupe/digits.html

Below is a scheme I have devised for memorizing the first 180 digits of Pi. The digits are split into two pages, with each page having seven lines (sentences). Consider each set of numerals in a sentence to be a word.

180 Digits of Pi – Memorization Scheme	
Page 1	**Page 2**
3.14159 26 5358	211 706 798 214
979 323 84 6264	8086 5132 8230
3383 2795 02884	664 70938 446
1971 69399 375 105	0955 05822 3172
820 974 9445 9230	5359 4081 2848
781 640 628 620	11174 50284 10270
899 862 8034 82534	1938 5211 0555

Practice the memorization in a cumulative, word by word, sentence by sentence style. Take the next step only when you can flawlessly recite the preceding digits.

Make four copies of this scheme, carry one with you and place the rest in convenient locations. Practice about four times a day for three to four minutes. With dedication, you will be able to attain your target within three to five months.

If mathematical clubs were to hold intra and inter school annual competitions, the current paltry African record of 661 digits could be extended five-fold or more within a few years.
The first 1,000 digits of π are given below:

1000 Digits of Pi

3.
141592653589793238462643383279502884197169399375105820974944592307816406286208998628034825342117067982148086513282306647093844609550582231725359408128481117450284102701938521105559644622948954930381964428810975665933446128475648233786783165271201909145648566923460348610454326648213393607260249141273724587006606315588174881520920962829254091715364367892590360011330530548820466521384146951941511609433057270365759591953092186117381932611793105118548074462379962749567351885752724891227938183011949129833673362440656643086021394946395224737190702179860943702770539217176293176752384674818467669405132000568127145263560827785771342757789609173637178721468440901224953430146549585371050792279689258923542019956112129021960864034418159813629774771309960518707211349999998372978049951059731732816096318595024459455346908302642522308253344685035261931188171010003137838752886587533208381420617177669147303598253490428755468731159562863882353787593751957781857780532171226806613001927876611195909216420198989

References:

1. Foer J (2012) *Moonwalking with Einstein: The Art and Science of Remembering Everything*, Penguin Books, New York.

2. O'brien D (2016) *You Can Have an Amazing Memory*, Watkins Media, London.

3. Blatner D (1999) *The Joy of Pi*, Walker Books, New York.

4. The comprehensive website www.joyofpi.com

On the issue of scientists and societal activism, see Albert Einstein's 1949 essay *Why Socialism?* reproduced at https://monthlyreview.org/2009/05/01/why-socialism/

BANANA READINGS

1. Chapman P (2009) *Bananas: How the United Fruit Company Shaped the World*, Canongate, New York.

2. Eagen R (2005) *The Biography of Bananas (How Did That Get Here?)*, Crabtree Publishing Company, New York.

3. Frank D (2005) *Bananeras: Women Transforming the Banana Unions of Latin America*, South End Press, Boston.

4. Frundt HJ (2009) *Fair Bananas!: Farmers, Workers and Consumers Strive to Change an Industry*, University of Arizona Press, Arizona.

5. Hanson M (2017) It's bananas to chuck out perfectly good fruit, *The Guardian*, 16 May 2017 (www.theguardian.com)

6. Koeppel D (2008) *Banana: The Fate of the Fruit That Changed the World*, Plume, New York.

7. Schlesinger S and Kinzer S (2005) *Bitter Fruit: The Story of the American Coup in Guatemala* (revised and expanded edition), David Rockefeller Center for Latin American Studies, Harvard University Press, Cambridge, MA.

8. Moberg M (2010) *Slipping Away: Banana Politics and Fair Trade in the Caribbean,* Berghahn Books, New York.

9. Sauco VG and Robinson JC (2010) *Bananas and Plantains (Crop Production Science in Horticulture),* 2nd Edition, CABI, New York.

10. Soluri J (2006) *Banana Cultures: Agriculture, Consumption and Environmental Change in Honduras and the United States,* University of Texas Press, Texas.

For a list of websites relating to bananas, see the Banana Basics section.

Street Vendors in Tanzania

The situation of street vendors and hawkers in the towns and cities of Tanzania has been well depicted in a series of investigative reports in a local daily, *The Citizen*. Some of these reports, available at www.thecitizen.co.tz, are listed below.

1. Kamagi D (2016) Do not harass small traders, Magufuli says, *The Citizen* (Tanzania), 12 August 2016.

2. Musa J (2016) Relief for street vendors after JPM orders stop to evictions, *The Citizen* (Tanzania), 12 August 2016.

3. Matandiko K (2016) Young people turn to hawking as poverty bites in Tanzania, *The Citizen* (Tanzania), 21 August 2016.

4. Editorial (2016) Ilala mayor has a point, but streamline trading, *The Citizen* (Tanzania), 4 September 2016.

5. Kimboy F and Musa J (2016) JPM halts eviction of traders, miners, *The Citizen* (Tanzania), 7 December 2016.

6. Malanga A (2017) Hawkers bring shopkeepers to their knees as rivalry bites, *The Citizen* (Tanzania), 26 January 2017.

7. Kimany G (2017) Mwanza authorities and hawkers: a catch-22 situation, *The Citizen* (Tanzania), 27 February 2017.

8. Kisembo D (2017) Order not to evict hawkers, vendors confuses officials, *The Citizen* (Tanzania), 27 February 2017.

9. Malanga A (2017) Municipal leaders say no areas for hawkers, *The Citizen* (Tanzania), 28 February 2017.

10. Nachilongo H (2017) How Ilala municipality grapples with problem of vendors, *The Citizen* (Tanzania), 28 February 2017.

11. Ubwani Z (2017) Arusha authorities in dilemma over hawker handling, *The Citizen* (Tanzania), 1 March 2017.

12. Malanga A (2017) What traders see as a major hindrance to business, *The Citizen* (Tanzania), 2 March 2017.

13. Malanga A (2017) Vendors 'to be evicted after improvement of new areas', *The Citizen* (Tanzania), 2 March 2017.

14. The Citizen Reporter (2017) Why dealing with hawkers requires long term strategy, *The Citizen* (Tanzania), 3 March 2017.

15. Malanga A (2017) Open markets neglected in Dar, *The Citizen* (Tanzania), 4 March 2017.

ACKNOWLEDGMENTS

Emma Hirji-Johnson provided perceptive comments and good suggestions at all the stages of the development of this book. It has also benefited from the comments of Rosa Hirji, Rafik Hirji, Yusuf Ahmad, Farida Hirji, Johnson John and Firoze Manji.

About two thirds of the photos appearing in this book were taken by my research assistant, Yusuf Ahmad who also provided typing assistance. My conceptualization of the Banana Pi was rendered into two elegant photos by Barnabas Mkwayu.

Warren Reed's expert editing has served to iron out the linguistic blemishes and errors that had crept into the work. His specific and general comments helped improve its literary quality. The editorial and design team at Mkuki na Nyota have done a superb job in producing an appealing final book.

Farida Hirji, my life partner, gave me untiring assistance in these days of compromised health and enabled me to continue my writing work. Further, as I gave dictation, she patiently typed a significant portion of the manuscript.

All of them have my profound gratitude.

AUTHOR PROFILE

Karim F Hirji is a retired Professor of Medical Statistics and a Fellow of the Tanzania Academy of Sciences. A recognized authority on statistical analysis of small sample discrete data, the author of the only book on the subject, he received the Snedecor Prize for Best Publication in Biometry from the American Statistical Association and International Biometrics Society for the year 1989. He has published many papers in the areas of statistical methodology, applied biomedical research, the history and practice of education in Tanzania, and written numerous essays on varied topics for the mass media and popular magazines.

He is the author of *Exact Analysis of Discrete Data* (Chapman and Hall/CRC Press, Boca Raton, 2005), *Statistics in the Media: Learning from Practice* (Media Council of Tanzania, Dar es Salaam, 2012) and *Growing Up With Tanzania: Memories, Musings and Maths* (Mkuki na Nyota Publishers, Dar es Salaam, 2014). He also edited and is the main author of *Cheche: Reminiscences of a Radical Magazine* (Mkuki na Nyota Publishers, Dar es Salaam, 2011). His most recent book is *The Enduring Relevance of Walter Rodney's How Europe Underdeveloped Africa* (Daraja Press, Canada, 2017).

He resides in Dar es Salaam, Tanzania, and may be contacted at kfhirji@aol.com.

Printed in the United States
By Bookmasters